BEYOND THE WITHERED ROOTS

MOIRA ESPINOSA
ALASTAIR RAPER
ALYS HALL
EL ROSE
MATTHIAS BOLATA

Barnard Publishing

If I Should Wake Before I Die copyright © Moira Espinosa
Bloods Call copyright © Alastair Raper
Arianrhod copyright © Alys Hall
Casting In Blood copyright © El Rose
That Which Follows You Back copyright © Matthias Bolata

Illustrations by Liz Ponting

ISBN 978-1-7395845-0-4

Barnard Publishing
Mold, Wales

becca@barnardpublishing.com
barnardpublishing@gmail.com

www.barnardpublishing.com

Contents

IF I DIE BEFORE I WAKE

MOIRA ESPINOSA

As a devourer of books and creator of worlds, Moira Espinosa seeks to spread fantasy through her own works of poetry and prose. She is currently an international student working toward her Master's in Creative Writing at Bangor University.

To insomniacs everywhere...

7 June 2018

THE BELOW REPORT EXAMINES THE MYSTERIOUS CIRCUMSTANCES of the investigation into the death of Eve W. Lars. The psychotic break down of Detective Inspector Daniel Jacobs, who was previously handling the case, has meant that this investigation remained incomplete and much of the evidence has been scattered. I am adding to this file as I sort the evidence that survived the fire earlier this year (hoping this means the station will go digital!). DI Jacobs's original notes were lost in the fire, although the original evidence reports are being recovered and added to this file. Preliminary reports suggested the cause of death was an accidental overdose, but DI Jacobs had disagreed. The investigation will be starting from scratch with my own analysis.

– DI Lucy Feran

EVIDENCE MARKER 1: DIGITAL LETTER
Details: The below letter was found on the computer of one deceased Eve W. Lars. The computer was not gathered as evidence in the original investigation as the death was ruled an accidental suicide. The below letter was found by the estranged sister of the deceased who insisted the death be investigated.

Analysis: It is likely most of the contents are a manifestation of severe, untreated mental illness. The investigation into the truth of this account is ongoing and will be put into context with the evidence collected by DI Jacobs.

JANUARY 17TH, 2018

I write this as a confession, an autobiography, and a goodbye. I don't expect I will wake up in the morning, although I will be really happy not to die. I thought my demon was just a nightmare, but now I know better.

I am typing this letter as my hands have been shaking too much for me to hold a pen. I'm not quite sure if my body knows and is afraid, or if it's the withdrawal again. I'm sober right now, but I wasn't always. I ask that you not judge me for that yet, not until you have finished reading this. I've really tried to get better. I expect my body will be found eventually, and hopefully someone will care enough to investigate the death of an addict. I'll leave my computer unlocked and plugged in to make it easy for someone to look.

I liked going to bed drunk because I didn't dream. I've been an alcoholic for a few years, and I always knew I was driving myself to an early death. As I write this, I'm twenty-six. I guess I'm just one of those people that was always going to die young. The problem was just that each time I tried to sober up, each time I did my best, called my sponsor, called my parents, I would start dreaming again.

The only time I really prayed was when my sleep paralysis would begin. I think I would wake up because I can feel when it watches me. It leans over me, laughing at me. It knows I can't move. It reaches for me, and I can't even cry. It can see me trying; I know it sees this in my eyes because it laughs.

It's taunting me.

I was thirteen the first time it visited. I was trying to take a nap in the afternoon, the sun peeking through closed blinds, when there was something in my periphery. It slunk out from under my bed, between the wall and the window, and it was smiling. I couldn't see it well and I tried to turn. I couldn't move my head. Well, at this point I could, sort of. I would turn my head, but it kept snapping back before I could look fully. I've never been someone who felt out of control of my body and I'm very stubborn, so I kept trying. It felt like hours. This thing was between me and the window, and I could hear my sister and her friends outside, laughing and playing. It was some vague shape of black and red, with white, white teeth. I got more and more panicked as my body refused to move, and then I saw it smile: the first time I heard its laugh.

It was a horrible sound. Piercing and high, like my ears were ringing, like I imagine a dog whistle sounds to dogs. I was sure that my ears were bleeding; they felt hot from the inside.

I woke up crying, sweating, and my room was the same way I had dreamed it. I jerked up as I woke, my body finally obeying me. I felt my ears, dry and a normal temperature. The sun was leaking through the blinds, and there was my sister laughing outside. There was nothing next to my bed. I yanked open the blinds to make sure that Faith and her friends were fine and they were, just chasing each other around the yard. The sun was setting. It was barely down, spreading golden light across the neighbourhood. I calmed down easily. I thought then that was the end of it.

Now, I try to scream. The last time, I could hear myself breathing through my nose, my mouth refusing to move. Have you ever felt that? Your body disconnected somehow from your brain, and you are a voyeur unable to make anything happen, no response from your body even as your mind screams at it to move. The feeling is somewhere beyond helplessness. When you feel helpless, it's easy to accept your situation, easier, at least. The creature that visits me evokes some primal instinct, some deep-rooted fear in the basest parts, something that won't let me calm, only lie there, screaming inside myself.

After last night, I know I'm on the precipice of something, between it and me. I don't think it's playing anymore. I'm afraid. I have to write this because if I don't wake up tomorrow, if it gets whatever it's wanted from me, I don't think that means everything is over. I think it just likes to play with its food. I guess this is more than everything I said before; I write this as a warning.

EVIDENCE MARKER 2: CONTENTS OF THE BIN

Details: The contents of the bin were influential in the decision to rule the death of Lars an accident. Among the items found were two empty 700ml bottles of whiskey, (one Jameson, one Writer's Tears), two empty boxes of Ibuprofen (16 tablets per pack, 200mg per), four empty and unlabelled prescription bottles, several full packets of instant coffee, food scraps, several takeaway containers from various restaurants, used tissues, and one bloody tea towel (analytics forthcoming).

Analysis: The deceased was a known alcoholic and a chronic narcotics and caffeine addict when not drinking, according to friends and family members. The mother of the deceased claimed their sobriety; however, the last person (landlord collecting rent) to see the deceased said they seemed erratic, twitchy, and had dark circles under their eyes. The behaviour is consistent with one abusing substances, but the landlord also significantly noted that the deceased did not smell of alcohol. The blood on the towel is being tested to confirm that it belonged to the deceased. The autopsy results and lab results have not yet been located and it is possible they burned.

Preliminary report of the officers who arrived on scene with EMS and investigated the scene states that the cause of death was clear after examining the apartment. The deceased was clearly suffering from psychotic delusions, as they had salt lining all doorways and windows, and all mirrors were covered with cloth decorated by religious symbols. They found the altar in the bedroom most disturbing, although I have not yet been able to locate photographs of this. The clothing of the deceased also seemed to be covered in oil, and a mostly empty bottle of chrism was found in the bathroom. After discovering the contents of the garbage, it was simple to conclude that the deceased had relapsed and OD'ed. It is not uncommon for addicts to deceive family and friends about their sobriety. I am fairly convinced that the deceased had a cocktail of pills and drink that ended their life, despite what DI Jacobs had claimed. Perhaps DI Jacobs's inability to accept this truth was the first sign of his impending breakdown.

I think maybe that some part of me always knew this thing would kill me. Maybe all the other shit was my subconscious trying to take control, to kill me before it had a chance to.

I started to dream, vividly, even when it didn't appear. I would dream of the same dead forest in black and white, and a house that I would find there. I was just fifteen the first time I found the house in the woods. There was a clearing in the trees and there the house stood, bone-white and silent. It was made of wood, two stories tall, with a wraparound porch that had an intricate and beautiful trim. The roof tiles were scaled, sloping gently to shade the porch and parting around an attic window. When I would first see the house, each time I dreamed it, I wouldn't remember the other times I had visited.

Actually, I don't think I would know at all except for my dream journal. As a side note, I am leaving this journal on my nightstand in my room in case I do wake up in the morning. I don't know if it knows that I ever kept track of its visits, or if it would even care, but I am noting here that the nightstand is where I have left it.

The house was pretty empty of furniture when I would walk in, a few large things but nothing that really said anyone lived there. My feet would leave prints in the dust that coated everything. I would head upstairs first. The stairs were grand and just to the right of the foyer and the bannisters carved into snake heads at each end, mouth open and fangs ready to sink into anything that got too close. I never wanted to touch them, but the floor had fallen through in several places and I had no choice. I wasn't sure what lurked in those holes, but I knew I didn't want to fall. The snakes were cold, but sometimes they would flex under my hand, only a brief movement. The air would feel thin upstairs, like I had climbed too high on a mountain. The bathroom was the first open door that I passed and there was something dripping from the ceiling. Without colour or memory, I didn't know what it was, and I stepped in to look at the puddle. It was just a dark stain on the tile floors, but I could see the reflection of the body on the ceiling.

It would take me a moment, but I recognised the face. Faith, my sweet sister, staring down at me from a ceiling too high for me to reach, dripping bright red from a gash on her throat. I screamed every time, sometimes outside of my dream, waking myself up and my family up.

When I wouldn't wake up, I would try to get her down. I tore through the house, looked for a stool, a ladder, something to help me reach her. She needed me, I had to help her. Somewhere in me I knew there was no one else, that I was the only one who could help her.

Some of the doors were locked but the attic door would always be open, the dropdown ladder inviting me up.

Note: Interestingly, DI Jacobs reported having strange dreams of a similar house shortly before his breakdown in February 2018. He was advised to take time off but refused. His mental health worsened; he survived the fire, and he had his breakdown and had to be hospitalised. It's entirely possible (perhaps likely) that the upsetting nature of this case was the catalyst in his breakdown.

I don't want to talk about the attic yet.

My parents decided it would be good for me to see a therapist for a while because obviously I was not sleeping well, and it was starting to affect all of us. I started meeting with Lily once a week, every Thursday at four after school. On our second meeting, she began by asking my mother for her payment, and then asking to be reminded of my name after my mother had handed her the check. Still, I was taken every week to a small office downtown and I'd sit on a couch and try to talk to Lily about life and try not to stare too hard at the portrait of Jesus she had on the wall behind her desk.

This Jesus, unsmiling, listened gravely as I spoke. He had deep circles under his eyes, which looked completely empty, as if the painter had run out of the bloody brown colour he was using. There were only faint circular marks framed by dark smudges and topped with slashes of dark brows. Jesus's temples were streaked with blood and his hair dripped with it. His expression felt accusing, like he was asking what I really had to be upset about when he was there with thorns digging into his scalp. I asked Lily about the painting and she said it was called 'Veronica's Handkerchief'. It was meant to look like the impression Jesus left on Veronica's veil, the imprint of his face as she wiped it before he walked off to Golgotha to die. The artist had certainly captured some haunting thing. I imagine it's difficult to see in your mind the way a person will look before they die, the sense of impending doom in their expression. I wonder if the artist painted Jesus's face first, and then added the details that make for this horrible thing, or if the horribleness of it was there from the first brush stroke.

I think of Lily now every time I see that painting. You may find it hard to believe, but I don't think that painting is a popular one for casual decoration, so now I only see it in my dreams. I hate it and it's horrible to look at.

That version of God heard all of the secrets I told Lily, every fear and nightmare I spilled from inside me. My mother would sit in the waiting room outside. She would collect me when my hour with God and Lily was up, and we would drive home in silence. I don't blame her for never asking me about the sessions; at the time I thought she didn't care, but now I wonder if she was actually trying to show some sort of respect for my privacy. Maybe she saw Jesus's face and just didn't want to know.

For a therapist, Lily wasn't very nice. She stared at me, forgot who I was, once she even spit. Not at me, I don't think, but at what I said. I haven't thought about this in years. I was telling her about that face that I couldn't really see. She spat and called me a coward. Lily thought I needed to face my fears. She said that I was holding myself back, that I should embrace every darkness inside myself, that it was the only way I could be whole. She said I had a demon riding my dreams, and I needed to let it in to get it out.

EVIDENCE MARKER 5: THE MOTHER'S TESTIMONY

Details: The mother of the deceased, one Samantha Marie Lars, testified to their sobriety and reported to having spoken to the deceased the day before their death. The deceased called them and chatted normally; the mother had no suspicion of any influences nor any inkling of possible suicide. The mother also confirmed that the deceased had a history of mental illness along with addiction, and provided the information of the deceased's childhood therapist, one Lilith Gordon, aka Lily.

Analysis: Again, it is not unusual for an addict to keep their substance abuse from their family. I am looking for Lilith Gordon's information to confirm if the deceased was at risk of suicide and to provide insight into the mental condition of the deceased.

My sessions with Lily ended after a few months. I had begun to resent my mother's silence and Lily's inability to remember my name, and that accusing gaze from behind her. I felt responsible for it all, since it was my screaming in the night that created this situation. I told them all that I felt better. Lily seemed happy to be rid of me.

After I stopped seeing Lily, I began sleeping with a towel in my mouth to muffle any kind of screaming. It worked well enough and my parents believed me when I told them I really was better. Faith knew, I think, but I locked my bedroom door and she could never come in to check on me like she did before when I had nightmares.

I've never in my life been loved like that except for her, and that's why I knew I had to keep her away. I was no good; something was always wrong with me, twisted. She was so good. I felt deep down in my heart that she was going to die because of me if I didn't stay away, an aching fear that some part of me would destroy her. I pushed Faith away. I was as cruel to her as I could stand; I just pretended she didn't exist. We haven't spoken in years now, but I check up on her sometimes. She's doing well, married to a nice man, has a good job. I knew she would be better without me.

All of this, whatever happens tonight, I'm facing it for her.

Faith, if you ever see this, I'm sorry. I should have done something else, something different that wouldn't have hurt you, that wouldn't have hurt us both. I was just a kid. Mom sent me off to someone else because she and dad didn't know what to do with me. I was too much for them, too wrong, too broken inside, and I thought I had to protect you from me. I'm sorry that I didn't get better. I'm trying now, for real, but I think I might be too late.

You might think I'm crazy at this point, and I really might be, but that doesn't mean it's not real.

I stayed away from home after school as long as I could. I met people, not quite friends, but people who didn't want to go home like me. We all had some sort of demon eating at us. I was sixteen when I first got drunk. One of the kids had an older boyfriend who bought us drinks and for the first time, I passed out and didn't dream. It didn't matter to me that I woke up with a headache and puking; I slept without dreaming for the first time in years.

I got away with it for a while before my parents figured it out. Since they both worked, they were too busy to notice if I snuck out of the house at night and came back drunk. Faith hated me enough then that she didn't care. They found out when I got caught stealing a bottle of vodka and I was almost grateful when they sent me to rehab. I was eighteen, maybe nineteen, then and I had pretty much forgotten what it was like to dream. I thought I might actually start to get better.

They moved me to my own room when the night terrors started again, and then put me on Valium. I don't remember much of that except that I loved the dizzy fog of it. I didn't feel anything bad anymore and I kept taking it when I left, until they refused to renew my prescription. I was twenty-one when I left, and twenty-two when I started drinking again.

The face came back, but this time it had hands.

EVIDENCE MARKER 4: RESULTS FROM BLOODY TEA TOWEL

Details: The blood from the aforementioned towel belonged to the deceased. The blood cells had not experienced significant oxidation and analysis indicated that blood was less than a day old. The amount of blood was substantial but far from life-threatening. It was also mixed with both saliva and stomach acid. There was no alcohol present in this sample.

Analysis: The lack of oxidation shows that whatever injury sustained by the deceased was extremely recent, occurring shortly before death. The presence of stomach acid and saliva in the sample could mean the blood was vomited; this should be confirmed by the examiner during autopsy. The lack of alcohol is particularly curious, given the empty bottles in the bin of the deceased. The question is raised then, of what the bottles were there for, of who may have drunk them. It seems unlikely that the deceased hosted any sort of party where others might have been drinking. Perhaps the deceased poured them out.

I can't remember a lot from the past few years. I was self-medicating again. I told my parents I enrolled in classes, and they believed me. They were so proud of me, finally. They thought I had really gotten better and that I had defeated whatever thing inside me that I'd been trying to drown. They've been sending me a monthly allowance, to pay for my "classes" and they pay my rent since I'm "a broke student." I think the landlord is an old friend of theirs, with the way she always checked in on me. If she does know them, she's kept my secrets.

She never told them that I rarely left, that this whole place used to reek of rotted grapes and the remains of alcohol sweating through my pores. I've cleaned it all now. If I go, I want to make it up to her. I even shampooed the couch cushions. I didn't even know you could do that.

I'm doing this for them too. Even though they didn't understand, I think they still loved me. They've really tried, even as I've failed them. Part of this is because of the last email they sent, asking if I needed money for graduation photos.

If I hadn't been how I am, I would be graduating now. I would have a degree in Theology and I'd be busy trying to plan my next phase. Instead, here I am, waiting for my dreams to kill me in my sleep.

The other reason is Faith, like I said. She sent me a wedding invitation last year, but this year, she's sent me ultrasound photos. She's having a baby. Even after years of me ignoring her calls, her texts and begging my parents not to get involved, she's still trying to include me in her life.

I don't deserve any of them. That's why I have to try now; I will fight this thing for her and for my parents and the niece I hope I get to meet.

EVIDENCE MARKER 3: PHOTOS OF THE BEDROOM OF THE DECEASED

Details: The bedroom of the deceased was rather filthy and unusual. While the living area seemed fairly tidy, the bedroom was covered in what seems to be dirt, and soil samples were collected and sent for testing. There was also some sort of altar on the desk of the deceased. There were several burnt out candles, which may account for the smell of burning that hung in the bedroom. The candles surrounded a mural which seemed to be a depiction of the Christian Jesus. Closer examination revealed that this mural was made with some sort of charcoal or ash, though neither was found in the apartment of the deceased.

Analysis: I have not yet come across the results of the soil samples and why DI Jacobs thought it important to collect the samples is unclear to me at this point. The mural seems to be a crude reproduction of 'Veronica's Handkerchief' which was previously mentioned in the digital letter. The dream journal that the deceased claimed to have in their letter also seems to be missing. It is not anywhere in these photographs, nor has it been located as evidence. It is possible that the psychotic state of the deceased caused them to misplace this journal, or perhaps it did not exist at all.

I've cleaned this place with sage as well as soap. I'm going to bless myself with the chrism before I to to sleep and I've lined the entrances and exits with salt, even though I think that is just for ghosts, not demons. I remember some old lady also saying that mirrors are gateways for demons, and I should have known better than to call her crazy, since I'm trying her methods now too. The rehab centre told me that hallucinations can be part of withdrawal, so I'm not sure if what I've seen in the reflections is real or not. Better to be safe than sorry. I'm covering them up.

I've been thinking about going to confession, asking God to forgive me for only talking to him when I'm afraid I might die. I went to church this morning. I walked up that aisle with the crowd of strangers, and I took communion even though technically I shouldn't have because I hadn't gone to confession. I'm hoping God will forgive me anyway. Out of everyone, I think He might forgive me. I hope it might help to have a piece of Him with me tonight, something to make me feel less alone. His presence with me might help me to break free from this...thing.

It waits for me in the attic. There's a ladder that drops down, and I climb it hoping to find another one, one I can take to the bathroom so I can reach Faith. It's dark up there. I fumble around, trying to feel what's around me until my eyes adjust. Its laughter starts so quietly that I think it's the floorboards squeaking under my feet, then it gets louder, and shrieking, and the way out disappears. The attic opening just disappears and I'm trapped in the dark, my sister beneath me, and both of us are alone.

In the time after Lily, I started seeing that awful painting in the attic. The way out would disappear, and the laughing would begin, and there were candles that would flare up around me in the darkness. They burned, hotter than they should have been for their size. They lit around that face; maybe they burned it to the ceiling themselves. It was Jesus again on His way to die, staring down at me in that blaming way of His. He stared, and the thing laughed, and I knew Faith was below me, bleeding.

AUTOPSY REPORT

The patient was a twenty-six year old Caucasian female. The EMS was called by the patient's landlord after she investigated a disturbance and found the patient without a pulse. Upon arrival, the EMS found the patient in their bed, smelling strongly of alcohol despite the landlord's insistence that the patient was a sober and recovering alcoholic. The smell was similar to isopropyl alcohol rather than drinking alcohol, and stung the eyes and noses of those on the scene. The patient was new to the area and thus had no medical history with the local GP. With no sign of a pulse or respiration and signs of decay, the patient was pronounced dead at the scene.

The EMS reported that the patient's body was significantly colder (27°C) than expected and rigour mortis had set in, although the landlord testified to having seen the patient alive approximately two hours before the emergency call. The landlord also testified that although the patient did not have a pulse, their eyes seemed to be tracking movement; the EMS declined to confirm this anomaly and stated that the landlord was hysterical and in shock. The landlord reported that the expression on the patient's face was 'unfamiliar'. The EMS reported that the patient's face had not yet relaxed and did in fact have a strange expression. One described the expression as 'accusing,' but the emergency worker in question is known to be superstitious (they also recommended a priest exorcise both the body and apartment).

External examination showed two third-degree burns circling each ankle of the patient. The burns are severe, and recent. They have not yet scarred, which means they are less than twenty-four hours old. There was bleeding in the ears, though the outside of them had been wiped clean of blood, and the left ear drum was completely ruptured. The patient also seemed somewhat malnourished and was experiencing hair loss around time of death, neither uncommon in patients with substance abuse problems. Although this was not noted in the EMS report, the coroner found that patient's tongue was missing from the body. It is likely the EMS did not perform a full examination on scene due to obvious signs of death.

Internal examination showed advanced scarring of the liver, but toxicology showed no blood alcohol content, and no evidence of opioid or narcotic intake. A full tox screen was completed to confirm the sobriety of the patient at their time of death. Of serious note was the discovery of the patient's tongue inside their stomach. The amputation of the tongue was done cleanly, with a single precise slice and no hesitation or teeth marks. There was a circular burn on the tongue with a cross in the middle, but it is unclear at this time what may have caused this burn.

Cause of death was sudden cardiac arrest, which is also not uncommon in the bodies of those who abuse substances. However, the sobriety of this patient is evident in the negative tox screen result. The cause of this cardiac arrest is undetermined.

Analysis: Based on the levels of rigour mortis and body temperature, time of death was estimated to be between 7-12 hours before the EMS arrived on scene. This was proven to be impossible as a hall camera corroborated the landlord's testimony and captured their interaction prior to the EMS call. The amputation of the tongue and sobriety of the patient also eliminates the possibility of an overdose as the cause of death. The way the body was cleaned of blood is also unusual, as it seems unlikely that the deceased would have cleaned their own blood as they died. It is now unclear to me how this death was ever ruled a suicide, even an accidental one, given the strange circumstances. At this point I believe the cause of death was not a suicide, and while Eve was clearly suffering from some sort of delusions, her paranoia may have been warranted by some actual threat to her life.

I find myself shocked at the sobriety of the deceased. Is it possible that someone tried to frame the death to look like an overdose? How did Eve swallow her tongue, and how was it cut off, and how was it branded? I am wondering if the bloody towel was used by whoever cut off Eve's tongue. If she choked on it as it went down her throat, that would explain the saliva and stomach acid found with the blood. Perhaps this person also used it to clean the blood from her ears. It is unclear to me if the deceased had any personal enemies who would attempt this. This could be the signature of a previously unknown serial killer and I have asked the admin to keep an eye out for any cases involving a similar signature. I am certain now that the same thoughts occurred to DI Jacobs, and that is why he had the soil samples collected from the bedroom. If the soil came from the shoes of this unknown enemy, knowing where they've been may help us to find them.

Last week, I poured everything out that I had, and I flushed every pill I had in the house. Most of it fit in the recycling but I put what didn't fit into the garbage can. I held out this time as my body adjusted. I made sure to eat even when I couldn't keep anything down, I didn't take anything for the pain even when my head felt like it was splitting from the inside, I showered and didn't re-wear any dirty clothes. The best part of withdrawal is that all the pain kept me awake for a few days. I got one night of actual rest before I started dreaming again.

I woke up yesterday without a fever, and I couldn't remember any dreams. It was one of the best days of my life. I cooked last night, drank only water, and called my mom before I went to sleep. I couldn't bring myself to tell her yet, that there was no need for graduation photos. That I've been lying to them for the past four years. I promised myself I would do it soon, and I will, I really will, if I wake up tomorrow. If I die tonight, I'd rather our last conversation not be an argument.

Mom, dad, if you see this, I'm sorry. I know how much this will hurt you to know I've been lying, that I've been telling you I'm better when I'm not and taking your money just to spend it on destroying myself. If you're reading this, I'm dead, but I want you to know that it's because I was really trying this time.

I'm sorry. I don't know how I'll fix everything, but if I make it through tonight, I promise I'll try. I want to be better. I'm trying.

14 JUNE 2018

I've been going through this case for a week now, trying to put all the pieces together. I called the institution where DI Jacobs was sent today. I wanted to check on him, but I also thought he might be well enough to talk a bit about this case. I find myself at a loss right now, without any clear leads and no answers for the Lars family, who've called asking for an update. It seems DI Jacobs has had to be kept sedated, as he repeatedly has woken in the night, inconsolable. He had been speaking of that same strange house in his dreams in the time upcoming and was insisting to doctors that some sort of demon was covering its tracks and set the fire that burned the evidence room here at the station.

While I know logically that this is impossible, that whether or not there is a such thing as demons, they would likely not have bothered to cover their tracks, I have found myself avoiding being alone in the dark. I am determined to remain as unaffected by this case as I am others, but this one is taking more out of me than I have expected. I have no update for the Lars family.

EVIDENCE MARKER 6: LILITH GORDON

Details: While Mrs. Lars was able to provide the contact information for Lilith Gordon, we have been unable to reach her, and the address provided by Samantha Lars is a construction site. It seems that the therapist's office building was demolished in 2014 to make space for a larger apartment building. The records of who rented space in the office building were located, but no one under the name Lilith Gordon, or Lily Gordon ever rented any of the spaces. The former owner had no record of any therapist offices in his building.

Analysis: This is unusual, to put it mildly. Clearly Samantha Lars recalls this therapist, as Eve does in her letter, and the father, Michael K. Lars has been able to provide records of the payments that were given to the woman. The only explanation I can think is that the woman was posing as a therapist and used a fake name. What would make her do this, for this specific child, is something I do not know, yet.

I went to sleep last night feeling like things might be okay this time around. I found myself back in that black and white forest, that world without colour except the red from Faith's veins. This time, the first time in four years that I had been sober enough to dream, I could remember that I had been there before. I played it out, the same way I always had, walking into that eerie and beautiful home and heading upstairs. I knew what was waiting for me in the bathroom, what I would find in the attic. For the first time, the snake banisters hissed at my touch as I climbed up. Their head turned as I walked and I felt theat, if not for the bars anchoring them to the steps, they might chase me down. I realised that they were imprisoned, like me, in this horrible place.

I wonder if they looked at each other the same way I looked at Faith when I saw her bleeding on the ceiling. Maybe that house is their hell as well as mine.

I went straight to the attic last night. I thought of my parents, Faith, the baby she carried. I wanted to be part of it again. Faith was trying to keep me in her life despite everything; my parents still dreamt a future for me, so I thought of them each step I took toward that attic ladder. I thought I was ready.

I climbed up, the air thin in my lungs. I was gasping by the time I reached the top. The candles were already burning and there He was, the terrible face of God's son looking at me, seeing every secret I've ever kept, every fear I've had. It was a physical weight, His gaze, so much that my knees gave out. The candles flared higher as I fell forward, choking. I was trembling so hard that my vision blurred, but maybe that was the smoke. The candles burned differently than they ever had and my eyes were watering when the shrieking laugh began. The candles were cold, sucking the heat out of the attic, and flamed higher as if the laughter was spurring them on, and then there was another noise, a different scream.

It took me a moment to realise that the sound was coming from just below me. The entrance to the attic had disappeared, the way it always did, but now I could hear Faith, screaming in pain or fear; I couldn't tell which. I could barely breathe, but I forced my feet under me. I stood and faced God above me.

I woke up in my bed. I realised it had been me screaming when I felt how raw my throat was. I was relieved for a lovely, brief, horrible moment. I tried to move, to grab the water cup from my bed, but my body didn't respond.

I was frozen, awake in my mind but my body slept around me. It rose at the foot of my bed, this creature that I've spent years trying to kill. A corpse from a grave, straight through the floor and leaving bits behind like it had torn its way straight through the ground up to my room. Its hands reached out and landed, burning my feet under its touch.

It's gotten bigger since the last time I saw it. The dark that made it was deeper than anything I've felt, and its teeth flashed bright white as it smiled. There was a flash of red as it opened its mouth and laughed. Its hands climbed higher, icy up my body and pausing at my shoulders as it hovered above me. I couldn't move; the only response from my body was the air panting through my nose. I could see my chest heaving as the thing moved closer. I saw its face clearly last night, for the first time since I was a child. I began the Lord's Prayer.

Accident Report: Electrical Fire

DI Jacobs was working late at the station the night of the fire on 2 February 2018. His desk is nearest to the evidence room, but his wife reported that he had recently not been sleeping well, which perhaps accounts for the fact that he slept through part of the fire.

The fire was caused by faulty wiring on the overhead light, which ignited and spread through the room unusually quickly. It is likely that the initial sparks landed on the clothes of Eve W. Lars, which had been soaked in oil and ignited quickly. The fire spread from there and the destruction is still being tallied. This unfortunate accident will set the station and the courts back months, as much of what was burned has not been digitalised. Any evidence that can be collected again, will be, but it's likely that many criminal cases will now be thrown out due to insufficient evidence. This setback not only delayed justice, but in some cases means a trial will not be possible at all.

DI Jacobs awoke to the smell of smoke and quickly pulled the fire alarm to initiate the sprinkler system. It seems the alarms in the evidence room had been installed incorrectly (along with the overhead light) such that they did not detect the room full of smoke and had to be manually activated.

Accident Report: Honourable Discharge of DI Daniel Jacobs

DI Jacobs suffered from severe lung damage from inhaling smoke before he woke and was hospitalised for recovery. Just after his release from the hospital on 5 February 2018, DI Jacobs went home and trapped himself in his upstairs bathroom. He locked himself in and refused to allow his wife (Ruth A. Jacobs) to open the door. She waited to phone the station until the following day, as she was convinced he would relent after a few hours of being trapped. Mrs. Jacobs phoned the station that morning after he had not emerged. Officers arrived at the scene and forcefully entered the bathroom, where they found DI Jacobs mumbling in his bathtub. He was speaking incoherently about a black and white house where a creature had trapped his wife.

Despite attempts to persuade DI Jacobs back to reality, he remained trapped within his delusions. DI Jacobs was sedated and taken for psychiatric care. He was honourably discharged from the service after being diagnosed with psychosis and early onset dementia. He has since been unable to recognise his wife nor any of his co-workers. DI Jacobs's delusions have invaded his sleep more than his waking life and he is under constant supervision lest he cause harm to himself or others. His medication has been extremely beneficial in his recovery, and he is being weaned off it as of June 2018.

Note: After the interference of DI Lucy Feran, an old co-worker of DI Jacobs, his recovery has taken a sharp decline. His hallucinations are more serious, and he has been refusing his anti-psychotic medication. He seems determined not to sleep as well and will only do so if sedated.

Its teeth were almost human, but the canines too long, the front two teeth sharpened to points and its eyes, white, no pupils only white with streaks of red racing through, bloodshot. It had no horns, and any tail would have disappeared in the inky black it wore. It was the black smoke that you might see in a forest fire burning too fast, but it was so cold. It swam in the air around this thing, this face that leered over mine. Its tongue, blood-red to match its gums, flicked out as it laughed at me.

The sound was just as it always had been in my dreams. The sound that made me flinch at every chair squeak, every car brake, like nails ripping through a chalkboard to scratch the wall underneath and filled with glee. It was a screaming, malevolent joy that tore through my brain. My ears burned, the same way they had the very first time. Its hands reached to my scalp and yanked my head back. I still couldn't make my mouth open to scream. I prayed inside my head, since my tongue would not obey me. I said the Lord's Prayer, the Hail Mary, a Glory Be, over and over in my mind.

I begged God, thought of Jesus and His glaring eyes and I tried to beg for help.

I think I passed out. When I woke up this morning, there was blood crusting my ears, and my ankles have burn marks, in the shape of those hands. Parts of my hair were torn, ripped from my scalp cleanly from the root. I was shivering, this time I think from cold and not withdrawal. Something about the smoke in the creature, it burned cold.

I went to church today. I've cleaned the place, written this letter, and I think I have to sleep. I've been avoiding this for so long; I know I have to face it even if it kills me. I'll never be rid of it if I don't try tonight. I don't know if I'll wake up, or if anyone will find this letter and know what I've been facing.

I think I can feel God with me today. He will give me strength; I'm hoping He will hear my prayers tonight. If I wake tomorrow, I'll go to confession. I'll talk to the priest, and then I'll call my parents to apologise. I'll send an email to Faith; I'll call her if she'll let me.

If I survive tonight, then I know I can fix it all.

Note: I've been having trouble sleeping. I'm thinking of passing this case to someone else, since I haven't been able to keep myself out of it. I find I'm dreaming of a black and white forest these nights. It must be the case getting to me; it's been too long since I've had a vacation, and my girlfriend says I've been thrashing in my sleep. I need rest, but I don't find peace in my sleep. I fear those woods, the darkness in the forest and what might exist within. I'm worried I will find the same house. Daniel couldn't take it, and neither could Eve. It might be real, it might not. I'm not sure it's worth the risk of wandering.

I'm requesting a few weeks off tomorrow. I don't want this case on my desk when I get back, though I know it will be waiting for me. I'll deal with it then.

--DI Lucy Feran

Bloods Call

Alastair Raper

Alastair Raper is a writer from Shropshire in England. He has loved reading fantasy and sci-fi books for as long as he can remember and is currently working on a collection of short horror stories. His previous publications include the short story Whispers on the Wind in the anthology Beneath the Poisoned Roots and Scarlet Warrior in the Literary Magazine, Sonder.

To all my family and friends who have supported my writing and helped bring this story to life.

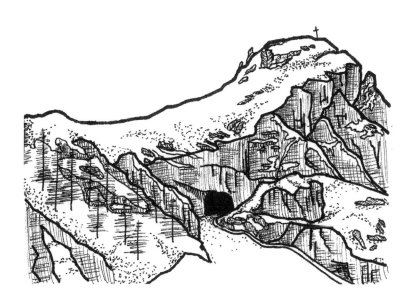

I REMEMBER IT AS IF IT WERE YESTERDAY, ALTHOUGH IN TRUTH IT feels like a lifetime away now and is rapidly fading.

"Inior, come along, quickly now!" My mother tugged at my arm, pulling me along the rough cobbled road that led to the base of the Rock, the immense mountain top monastery of the Covenant of Hema.

"It's such an honor," she was saying as we went, "a calling is only heard of once or twice in a lifetime. For one of our family to have a chance to join the ranks of the Covenant is a great thing and, if you are chosen it may help you control some of your...powers." My mother paused as she said the final word, almost spitting it as though it left a bad taste in her mouth. I couldn't help but notice that, as if by instinct, she also flexed the withered, ruined remains of her right arm and a sliver of guilt speared through me as I saw the handiwork of a previous demonstration of my power. It was this, I think, the knowledge that as I grew older, my growing powers would become harder to contain, as well as the handsome amount of silver coins with which she would be compensated, that led my mother to bring me to the dark shadows of the mountain on the day of the Calling.

We weren't the only ones making our way to the base of the mountain that morning. As we'd left the sun behind us and fallen under the mountain's looming shadow, we were joined on the road first by a few others, the families of others from our village and the neighboring hamlets. But by the time we were close enough to see the crack in the rock face that marked the only way into the monastery, the crowd around us had grown to numbers many hundreds strong. With each group I saw children, many who looked younger than me but some who looked almost as old as sixteen. So many families willing to give up their own blood to the Covenant. I understood little at the time of what the adults whispered at night, but I could see that some days there were fewer pieces of bread to go around, and I'd not had a scrap of meat in a week. All of us making this walk were painfully thin, even the groups that joined us from the roads to the south, each of them wearing robes of bright silk that seemed to glitter even without sunlight. For a second, I could think that this was a kindness of my mother, for to be chosen by the Covenant would mean warm food and a place to sleep rather than shivering under thin blankets.

"Come along!" she barked again and tugged my arm and the thought fled as, even to my young mind, I could tell she was thinking of the extra portion of food she could spare herself this evening.

A short while later, the front our group had made it to the dark crack in the cliff and our pace slowed as we waited patiently to enter. As the entrance grew closer, I took a final look around at the countryside surrounding the lone mountain for a final time. Away from the chill of the shadow cast over us, the sun was blazing down against the forests that covered the hills rising from the dirt to compete with the Rock. I tried to imagine the warmth of that sunlight flowing through me as the we entered the cliff face and for a few brief seconds were entirely swallowed by darkness. But I felt nothing save the cold dampness of stone.

We walked in darkness for a time with only my mother's shadowy back and her hand still in a vice like grip around my arm to show me the way. I was beginning to wonder how long we would continue like this, how far we had traveled into the belly of the mountain when the space around us abruptly opened into a large cavern lit by the flickering glow of orange torches. The space we entered was vast, easily capable of holding the procession that now streamed into it. I could see a low wooden fence before us, splitting the cavern into two semicircular areas, the second of which was only accessible through a narrow gate which stood directly ahead of me. At a glance they looked more like enclosures to hold livestock than people. As we assembled in the first of these spaces, each of our faces turned to a raised platform at the far end of the second pen where three figures covered completely in red robes stood.

As all of us watched, from the middle of the group stepped forward a figure with their arms raised to the sky. The robes covered their entire body and though I strained my eyes to see under the figures hood, I saw only an empty void of darkness. Then they spoke, their voice a whispering rasp as though two sheets of parchment were being rubbed together. The voice sounded old, ancient even although it was unmistakably female.

"I am Reverend Mother of this holy place and I bid you welcome to the caverns of the Covenant of Hema. Step forward those of you who would be seen worthy to join our number, come." As she spoke, the Reverend Mother's robes shifted in a motion that I could only think of as beckoning. I found myself being propelled forward, half by the hand of my mother and half by the movement of those around me as they too were pushed away by those who had brought them here. We moved as one towards the gate that separated the two pens. Before I could fully register what was happening, I found myself standing at the foot of the raised platform surrounded by tens, if not hundreds, of children all of us looking up at the red robed figures, two of whom were now making their way down steps at the side towards us.

"Brothers Lorez and Miko, our Shepherds of Novices will now inspect your offerings," whispered the Reverend Mother from her place atop the platform and I looked around, confused, for I had no offering to give. Neither, it seemed, did any of the others who pressed around me for I saw confusion on their faces also. It was as the two robed monks reached the first of us that I realised the Reverend Mother had not been speaking to us at all. We were the offerings being presented.

They were moving between us now, faces, hidden by deep

hoods, passing from one frightened looking child to the next. Occasionally they paused by one and seemed to stare intently at them with eyes that were hidden in shadow. I don't think I heard any sound come from them at all, save the low swish of their robes as they drifted through us. Then one was before me, Lorez or Miko, I had no idea. It stared at me with that black void for a long time and I tried to stare back, mustering all the strength I had, though my mind screamed at me to run back to my mother. That she had dragged me to this place herself was of little consequence now. But I was frozen to the spot by the eyes that I could feel, rather than see, studying me intently.

And then, with a sudden rustling of robes, its hand shot out to grab me by the chin. Old did not describe the look of the arm that I could see. The skin was wrinkled and cracked, scored through with webs of dark veins that wrapped tightly around the outlines of bones protruding up through its sunken flesh. Now I wanted to scream but the vice-like grip of its bony hand kept my mouth from opening. It twisted my head from left to right so hard I thought my neck might break and I waited to hear the shouts of protest from my mother, or indeed any of the adults arrayed in the enclosure behind us, but no sound came at all. Even the children around me, though I could see they had recoiled, were silent. Then, as quickly as it had grabbed me, the monk let me go and moved past me to another child. I shuddered as its robes brushed against me and I felt a strong metallic smell invade my nose, although at that point I could not identify it.

It seemed an age until the monks, these Shepherds of Novices as the Reverend Mother had called them, had made their way through the entire crowd and rejoined her on the platform. I was still shaking from my experience with them and the others around me were eyeing me warily for I had seen no one else be grabbed in such a way. My nervousness was increasing, and I felt my fingertips tingle with power in response. I willed it to stop, trying to push away the feelings rising in me.

Upon the platform the monks seemed to be talking to the Reverend Mother; the shape of their robes suggested that their heads were inclined towards her but if they were speaking, I could hear no sound. This entire ordeal had been conducted in the deepest silence. As I looked up at her, trying to hear what was being said, the Reverend Mother's robed head turned so the darkness of the hole that hid her face was pointed directly at me. Despite her distance from me I froze, as I had when the monk was standing before me, and I felt as though my blood was freezing in my veins and slowing to the most minute crawl through my body. The tingle of power in my fingertips was gone, almost as though it had been sucked away by her gaze.

For what could have been an eternity I held her hidden gaze before her hood shifted back to look over all of us and I felt my blood begin to run in my veins again. Once more the Reverend Mother stepped to the edge of the platform and raised her arms to address the congregation behind us. Again, her whispered voice carried clearly on the air.

"Hear me, all of you faithful. Be honored for your offerings, for we have found them all worthy to join with us as a part of our Covenant." She gestured and a before unseen corridor in the rock was revealed as the torches that surrounded it burst into flame.

"Through there you will receive our thanks for the new blood you have brought to us, although I must caution you that, from the moment they enter our sacred halls, your offerings are a part of the Covenant, and you may have no further contact with them." Whether the majority heard her last words, I was unsure as they had started moving as one like a herd of cattle towards the hole in the rock, leaving us behind. Some of the younger ones cried out as they saw their parents leaving, perhaps unsure of what was happening. I was searching for my mother's face among the crowd, but if she looked my way as they rushed to collect their silver pieces, I do not know for I could not find her among the sea of jostling heads. And then we were alone.

The Reverend Mother and her companions had turned to face the rock wall behind them, and, with a great rumbling and cracking of stone, it began to rise revealing a great corridor beyond.

"Come." The Reverend Mothers words reverberated around us, the whisper penetrating deep inside my mind until I was sure it was emanating from inside my head. I felt a tug in my body and took an involuntary step forward. Looking around I saw that others had taken a step too and had looks of confusion on their faces. The tug came again, and it felt as though the very stands of my veins were being compelled to flee my flesh and follow this strange woman.

I cannot say how long we walked into the bowels of the mountain, or even with any accuracy what we saw. It was as if each of us were sleepwalking at the command of the red robed figures who drifted before us. I should have fought it; we all should, but in our minds, it seemed so clear this was the path we were meant to walk. The tug in my body guided me onward and when we arrived at a metal door that opened into another huge, dimly lit chamber, I followed my fellows inside and stood, still in the grips of this unnatural trance, watching the rest flow in and stand alongside me. I saw the last person to enter, a young boy, no older than ten I guessed, was stopped at the threshold. One of the thin, bony arms slipped out from beneath a robe to bar his way. At this he seemed to awaken from the trance and terror filled his eyes as he took in his surroundings. Without a word, the almost skeletal hand curled around his shoulder and turned him to face away from the door. Then he was gone, escorted away by the monks to, at the time, who knew where. Then the door slammed shut and we were left in the low, flickering light of the torches. The moment the door closed, the trance that held our minds slipped away and the realisation of what had happened flooded back. I tried to speak, to ask what was happening but my mouth wouldn't form words and, when I tried to take a step towards another member of our group, I felt the tug inside me again holding my body to that spot. At that point our minds were free, but it still felt like we were being taken prisoner inside our own bodies. There was panic on some people's faces, and I could feel it twisting within me like a serpent but, as before I tried to suppress it. Whatever this place was we found ourselves in, I could not let my powers go uncontrolled here in my panic.

It wasn't long before we heard the screeching of rusted metal hinges and the door swung open again. This time just one figure stood there. Whether it was Lorez, Miko, the Reverend Mother herself, or even someone new I could not tell for the same red robe covered them all. I saw this one stretch out an arm that looked darker skinned than the one I had seen before, although equally as aged and decrepit looking. Its hand beckoned with claw like fingernails and a girl to my left stepped forward and walked through the door which, again, slammed shut. From then on, every so often the door would screech open and another of our number would be taken away. I could see the fear growing in the eyes of those that remained with each other person that left. They were wondering, I knew, was it better to be one who was taken, or one who was left behind. Some even tried to resist, and their mouths were working in silent shouts and bodies twitching violently as they attempted to turn and run from the tug that we all knew was pulling them ever onward. Whether their reluctance concerned the figure in the door, there was no sign, for they simply stood watching their new chosen walk past before following themselves.

When there were only a few of us left, they came for me. A crooked, clawed finger beckoned in my direction and the tug in my veins was leading me out of the door. This time I did not enter a trance state and was able to take in my surroundings in more detail. I walked through hallway after hallway, each of monumental design and grandeur; intricately carved stone archways held up ceilings that rose to incredible heights and were covered in stained glass images, depicting what I guessed to be various gods and demons locked in a battle for the heavens. Through great doorways, I could see equally cavernous rooms, some of which looked to be hubs of activity through which red robed figures scurried although I could not tell their tasks. One looked to be a kind of chapel where a statue depicted a horned and winged figure was pouring some liquid into the mouth of a kneeling worshiper. Arrayed around the statue I could see the red robes of monks prostrate before it. The door to another room burst open and a line of figures bustled out, each carrying a large bucket, the handle to which disappeared up inside their robes. As I passed, they swung their hooded heads to look at me and, long after they passed, I imagined I could still feel their eyes boring into me. My legs were beginning to ache when I finally felt the tug subside and found myself standing in front of a door larger than any I had seen previously. It began to rumble open, and I felt the sharp, desiccated hand of a monk at my back, pushing me inwards.

The room I entered, like all those I had walked through, was cavernous. Hanging braziers lit a path down its center that led to a large dais, leaving the rest of the room to sink into pitch black darkness on either side. On the dais a fire crackled underneath a large metal sheet that I could see, as I slowly drew closer, held dark red disks of what looked like meat that sizzled and spat in the heat. To either side of the fire stood two more monks and, as I approached, one produced a metal spatula and scooped a single disc up and offered it, still steaming and spitting, towards me. All the time they watched me with that intense silence and stillness. I reached the bottom of the steps and warily held out my hand to take the circle of meat. It was still intensely hot to the touch and scalded my fingers as I gripped it. The monk gestured with the spatula, indicating that I should eat it. Raising it to my lips, I felt the strange metallic taste of whatever substance it was made from. I forced it down and it was as I swallowed the last mouthful that I heard, for the first time since the Reverend Mother had commanded us to enter the mountain, one of the monks speak.

"Be blessed," it croaked as the two of them raised the arms of their robes high, exposing yet more ancient, wrinkled flesh. "For your blood has been purified with that given by those thrice blessed from the one who walks beyond the veil"

"Praise him, harbinger of the red rain," intoned the other and they began to advance upon me. On an instinct, I tried to take a step back, but my legs felt heavy, and my vision swam before my eyes. I stumbled as they reached for me, and their arms seemed to twist and intertwine with their robes as a heavy drowsiness took hold and I fell seemingly forever into the blackness of sleep.

~

When consciousness returned to me, my first sense was that there was something moving around me. As feeling crept back to my body, I became aware that I was lying down on a cold, hard surface surrounded by the same strong metallic smell I'd experienced earlier. I could feel something tight wrapped around my left wrist and when I tried to move my arm to bring it to my face so I could see what it was, my arm refused to move, and I realised it had been bound to whatever surface I now lay on. Then I felt a tight pressure in my ankle as whoever was moving around me wrapped something tightly around it and bound that foot in place. My other limbs were free and had yet to be bound in place. Slowly, not wanting to alert whoever was binding me, I cracked my eyes open. There was a monk at the foot of the table I lay on. He stood there, robes rolled to his shoulders and hood flung back, gently smoothing a length of cloth he was surely about to use to bind my other foot. I should have reacted then, kicked out and struggled with my free limb but the fear that rose in me as I looked at a monk, now unmasked before me kept me frozen to the bed.

He was painfully thin with skin that looked yellowed with age like parchment that stretched taught over his bones. The fingers that held the cloth were long and ended in clawed nails like the ones that had collected us one by one from the chamber. As I watched his fingers deftly weave their way through the cloth, I saw that they seemed to bend and twist in odd ways, as if they had too many joints. I was sure then that my brain was playing tricks, still trying to recover from whatever they had drugged me with.

It was then I realised that he was speaking, mumbling softly under his breath as he began to wrap the cloth around my other leg that was still paralysed in fright. I tried to watch his lips move in that face that was little more than an animated skull and began to understand the words he was saying.

"Softly softly, don't let him awaken. Collect the blood, yes, the blessed blood, for him that walks unseen. Praise the red harbinger. But not for us this one. No. No. The Mother herself wants him. She sees what he has, what he will bring." I felt a cold, dry hand caress my leg then a sharp pain shot through my body causing me to bite my lip to stop myself crying out. He had sliced the razor-sharp tip of a knife along my leg and was holding it up to the candlelight. I saw a dark red drop collect at the end as he held it high in the air.

"Ahh, blood of power, so potent and," he let the drop fall and a long dark tongue flicked out and caught the drop midair and a shudder ran through his body, "so sweet." The monk laid his hand back on my leg.

"Be honored. You shall be the final one, the final blood of power to break the veil and bring forth the harbinger; praise him."

Leaving the knife by my feet, the monk moved to my other side where my final limb lay unbound. As he did, he pulled out a final length of cloth and I knew I had to act before I was completely helpless. I pushed against the fear holding me in place and felt it then, the tingle in my fingertips as my power rose to the surface again. This time, instead of fighting against it, I let it fuel me and found my previously paralysed limbs emboldened by the feeling that now flowed through them.

The monk was standing over me and I could see the wet gleam of his eyes set deep into the shadows of his sockets looking down at me and that black tongue rolled over his thin lips leaving a red smear behind them. His claw like hands reached for me and through my squinted eyes I could indeed see that his fingers bent at odd angles with more joints than any human should have.

In a sudden burst of movement my hand leapt up and grabbed him around his thin wrist. Just as years before when my mother had received a taste of my power, I felt the energy flow through me, and he screamed a shrill, coarse sound that felt as though it was tearing the back of his throat as we both saw the effect of my now directed power. The skin of his arms began to shift and crack as rivulets of dark, thick blood began to seep from between splitting skin. The monk tried to pull his arm away, the panic etched into his skull like a face as the skin withered and slipped away but I held firm, pouring as much of my power into him as I could. The skin surrounding his clawed fingers began to flay away, revealing white bones underneath that too began to crumble to dust.

The concentrated release of my fear kept my fingers grasped around the monks ruined arm, but I was so focused on my task that I failed to see his other hand swing around to strike at my face, and my lip split as my head was thrown back and my grip faltered, allowing him to pull away to the foot of the table, nursing what was left of his other arm. As powerful as I felt in that moment, I was still bound to the table by my other limbs and panic flared anew in my chest as I watched the monk seize the knife he had left at my feet and leap towards me while he cursed me.

"I'll flay you, you little maggot, I'll drain you while you're still living you…" His knife swing was clumsy, the pain of his destroyed arm, probably the only reason the knife didn't open up my throat. The blade missed me by a hair's breadth and struck the table, where it shattered and showered us both with shards of metal that cut into our skin alike. Then he was on me, leaping with startling ferocity for a person as ancient as he obviously was and had received a wound that would cripple a normal man. The long fingers of his remaining hand pressed hard into the sockets of my eyes and my eyes filled with a burst of pain and bright lights against the dark pressing down on them. I let out a scream of my own, flailing my free arm trying to dislodge him. By some piece of good fortune, my arm found his own face and, grasping it with my hand, I let my power flow through me again. My hand pressed hard into his face and I felt the sharp edges of his bone beneath a skin that had the texture of a thin incredibly dry parchment. After what seemed an age, I felt the pressure of his fingers on my eyes lessen then I felt the bone under my hand give way and he slumped forward, finally quiet and still. Without opening my eyes to see what remained of him, I twisted my body and used my hand to push the monk's dead weight off my chest.

I lay there for a while after that; I felt drained, and my fingers burned with phantom pain where they had released my power. It took an immense amount of strength for me to undo the binds that held my other hand, enabling me to sit up and see, for the first time, the room I was being held in. What I saw caused the last dregs of strength from my power to fade and that all-encompassing fear to return. The room was long and low, unlike the other chambers I'd seen inside the mountain and contained row upon row of stone tables identical to the one I lay on. Like mine, each table was occupied by a person, or as I guessed from the pale colour of their skin and the red stained tubes that led from their flesh to large buckets on the floor, a body. Many of them I recognised from those who had stood with me in the pens earlier for the calling and each had been drained of their blood. Horror ran through me as I finally realised what the metallic taste and smell I had been experiencing was. Looking down, I saw the same tubes and bucket beneath my table. It was only through luck that I had survived when so many hundreds of others had perished.

I remembered what the monk had said as he'd bound me. About my blood being only for the Reverend Mother due to the power it contained. I thought further back to the way one of the Shepherds of Novices had looked and reached out for me and the way the Reverend Mother herself had looked at me in the pens. Had they seen my power then? And what could they use my blood for? The monk had mentioned it being the final one to bring forth this harbinger I had heard them talk about. Whatever that was, I knew I couldn't let them catch me again.

I was shaken from my thoughts by the sound of an opening door and saw, beyond the field of bodies, a group of more red robed figures enter. Thankfully, they were still far from me, and I was able to roll myself off the table and land silently on the floor without them noticing. Despite the panic rising inside me, the fear of what they would certainly do to me were I to be discovered kept my mind focused and I slowly began to make my way between the tables keeping my head as low as possible. The monks, it seemed, were making their way through the room and from what I could see through hurried glimpses above the table, they were inspecting the bodies that they passed and pulling the tubes from them now their bloody work was done. They seemed very preoccupied by their work, and I began to move quicker towards the door and the beckoning orange light that lay beyond. I wasn't aware that I had been holding my breath for the last, heart pounding, rush across open floor to the door but, once I had slipped through it, my head swam with dizziness, and I let out a great gasp of air.

The corridor I had entered was smaller than the ones I had been compelled to walk down to receive the Covenant's drugged blessing. While the larger ones were supported by pillars decorated with statues and enormous hanging panes of stained glass, this one had a low ceiling and simple brickwork stretched away, lit by the light of wall mounted torches. The whole place had a practical, industrial feel that was lacking in the grandeur and splendor of the halls I had glimpsed so far and for some reason, that scared me far more than if it had emulated the rest of the monastery. At least then it would have seemed as though there were some ritual and symbolism in our deaths.

My first need was to find a hiding place to recover some strength. I made my way slowly down the corridor praying to whatever gods I still felt deserved my worship after this dark place's facade of holiness. I did not meet anyone as I crept along although the drops and smears of dark red liquid revealed on the floor by the torchlight suggested that this way was used often for transporting the useful parts of Covenant's victims. The corridor continued for a long way and with each of my steps that echoed off the walls around me, I was terrified in the silences that followed that I would hear another pair of footsteps echoing to signal the end of my brief freedom. Eventually I found what I had been looking for, a smaller tunnel that led off from this one to a staircase that wound up into darkness. It was beneath the staircase that I found a moment of safety. There was a small alcove deep in shadow that I crawled into and allowed myself to give in to the exhaustion that overtook me, and I fell into a deep sleep.

~

I awoke an unknown amount of time later; time had ceased to be meaningful in this place, far from where the light of the sun could reach. The ground was hard, and my body ached as I pulled myself to my feet. For a second, I hoped that the whole ordeal had been nothing but a nightmare, although a look from the alcove out to the dimly lit stairwell brought all of reality crashing back down. I had to find a way to escape. Something told me that the way I had come, if I could even find my back to those halls, would be closed to me. There were two choices before me, the corridor I crept along from that dreadful room of death or the staircase that wound its way up high above me. I chose the stairs as I thought the corridor offered far more chance of my capture and, quick as I could, I ran from the alcove and onto the first step, trying to leap out of sight of anyone who may have been walking past. I climbed the stairs for an age.

They wound upwards in increasingly uneven steps, and I realised the walls around me had changed again. Gone was the brickwork below and now the simple, rough feel of cut rock pressed into my fingers as I pulled myself onward. A part of me was relieved as it seemed increasingly unlikely that I would meet any monks but another part of me felt the pang of a rising fear that I would wander these dark passages until I collapsed from exhaustion. The darkness was close around me, very few torches lit this path and I scurried from shadow to shadow.

I must have continued in this way for some hours, continuing up the stairs or occasionally leveling out to allow me to catch my breath in a corridor. It was in one of these corridors that I saw a light shining from behind a large stone archway. I'd passed other rooms previously, all bathed in blackness and, unable to see what would have awaited me in the dark, I'd hurried on past. But now there was light, and, despite my fear of capture, I found myself drawn towards it.

The room beyond was large; its walls carried the same markings of rough carved stone and stalactites dripped from the high ceiling overhead but what made me pause and, for a second, regret my choice to enter, were the cages. They were made of thick iron bars and inside some of them I could see the shapes of people slumped against them. Upon approaching I realised that these people weren't alive. Some looked to have been lying here for months at least and I could see the flesh rotting away to reveal the white of bone underneath. Some of them looked to be wearing pieces of armor, although they were tarnished, and rust spotted with the drips from the stalactites overhead. I was turning to leave this place and continue to desperately try and find a way to salvation when I heard a gruff voice from behind me.

"Hey. You there." I froze, thinking for a second that I had been discovered, that a monk lurking among these cages of the dead had chanced upon me. Then the voice came again.

"Hey. Come here. Are you deaf?" I realised then that the voice carried none of the croakiness or age that I now associated with a member of the Covenant. I turned back to the room, searching for the source of the voice amidst the cages.

"Over here. By the desk, under the big stalactite." I'd found the source of the voice. There was indeed a stalactite, larger than the rest, that hung over a particular cage and in front of it, I found an abandoned desk with papers strewn over its surface. While I had taken this gaol to be full merely of corpses, upon coming into view of this cage I realised that there was still some-one alive in this place. He looked to be a man of middle age and, like some of the bodies I had passed, was wearing an armored breastplate although his still shone, as he stood against the bars of his cage in the torchlight, as though it were new.

"There you are. Now who are you lad? You're not one of them monks are you." It was a statement more than a question and I approached, a feeling of relief washing over me at having discovered another living being in this hellish place that did not seem to be actively trying to drain my blood for their own occult purposes.

"No sir, I was one of those presented to join the Covenant at the calling. They fed us something and I awoke as they were trying to drain my blood. I fought back and got away. I've been looking for a way to escape but it has only led me to you and, I fear, further from a way out." The words fell from my mouth in a jumble as my emotions took hold and I found myself trying to recount my entire horrific tale to this man I had only just met. As tears were stinging my eyes and threatening to course down my cheeks at the height of my verbal tirade, the man put his hand up to stop me and spoke again, although his voice was softer this time.

"It seems you've had a hard time here lad, much harder than even myself and my fellows," he gestured to the surrounding bodies, "but I need you to try and focus for a minute. There's a way we can both get out of here I'm sure but for now I need your help. Can you do that, lad?"

A shred of hope flared in me at his words. A way out, could it be true?

I nodded and stammered, "Of course, what do you need?"

"Over on that table," he gestured towards the desk that stood beside the cage, "there's some keys that the guard left behind. I'm not sure where he's gone but he could be back any minute so we must hurry."

I nodded and, drying my eyes, began to search the table for the keys. I found them wedged between two stacks of bound papers and brought them back to the man in the cage.

"Thank you, lad," he began to try the many keys in the lock at the door to his cage, "now my sword, they threw it over by those boxes." I crossed to the boxes and began to search as quickly as I could through and around them. I'd pulled out several sheets of sackcloth before I saw the glint of metal. My hand wrapped around the cool hilt of the sword and tried to tug it free. In my rush my hand slipped, and I fell backwards. Behind me I heard the click of a lock and whisper of relief from my new companion. Then as the silence returned to fill the gaps left by our noises, I heard the sharp tapping of footsteps against rock. I glanced, panicked, at the man in the cage, who had half opened his door, and he gestured to for me to hide while pulling the door closed again but, I noticed, keeping it unlocked. I pulled some of the sackcloths over myself and crouched down, trying to appear as though I were little more than a collection of cast-off material lying next to the boxes.

The monk rounded the corner, all of its body hidden by red robes save a gnarled hand that clutched a wooden mug tightly. I could hear its contents slosh with each step closer the figure took. It passed by the man's cage without so much as a turn of its hood towards him, rather, it pulled a worm-eaten looking chair from the shadows to the table and sat down, shifting aside some of the papers so it could place its mug. Then a second ancient hand appeared and, reaching up, it threw back its hood to reveal skeletal looking face, similar to the monk who had tried to drain my blood. I watched as it gazed down into the mug and a red stained grin split its face. Then it raised the mug to its lips and took a long gulp. The wrinkled, hanging flesh of its throat rippled as the liquid flooded down its throat and I saw a single stream of crimson begin to run from the corner of its mouth. Taking his chance, the man in the cage was moving. The door began to quietly swing open again as he pushed it and the monk, so preoccupied with gulping down his drink, didn't notice what was happening behind him. The man was inches away from being able to squeeze through and reach the monk. What he would do without a sword I had no idea but the idea of having finally found an ally pressed against my previous fear and hope flickered inside me.

And then the door squeaked. At once there was a blur of action. The monk whirled his head around so fast I was sure I heard the sound of cracking bones to face the man as he threw open the door and hurled himself at the robed figure. The chair went over, falling to the ground with a crash and splintering across the rock while the two of them sprawled on the ground close enough to me to stir the fabric I hid under. The monk found his feet first and, with a strength I could never have guessed he possessed, kicked the man in the ribs hard enough to throw him back against the bars of his cage. The monk steadied himself as the man rose once more to his feet and I felt a pressure in the air as a withered hand reached out to the mug that had been discarded on the table. The pressure built in my ears until I thought they would burst and then it was gone as the monk flicked his hand forward and a crimson shard shot from the mug to where the man had been seconds before. As it hit the cage, the shard broke apart, splashing as if it had become liquid again and I saw, where droplets had landed, faint wisps of smoke rising from them. The man too it seemed, though he had avoided much of the attack, had been hit and hissed in pain as he batted at the sleeve of his shirt where I could see holes being eaten away in the fabric. Where the liquid had hit the metal of his remaining armor, I was reluctant to call it blood after whatever sorceries the monk had performed on it, it dripped in sizzling red lines until it fell to splash on the floor.

The monk was reaching for whatever was left in the mug and I felt the pressure build again. I knew I had to do something. I summoned the fear, panic and pain I had felt earlier, and, in reply, my power began to tingle again in my fingertips. Keeping a grip on my power, I summoned the courage I could and threw aside the sackcloth covering me, leaping for the monk with my hands outstretched. My fingers closed around its shin and forced my power into him. It shrieked as, with the combined force of both my hands on his leg, the skin was instantly flayed to dust followed by the bones which yellowed, cracked and burst apart under my grip. He came down on top of me and I was lost in the musty, metallic smelling robes and the feel of his bones twisting as he thrashed about trying to right himself. I can only presume that the man took this opportunity to recover himself and reach his sword for the next thing I knew, a shaft of silver was sliding out of the back of the robes in front of my face. No blood sprayed as I would expect from a body that had just been impaled, but rather it slid in slow, thick droplets down the blade. Then the blade retracted, the body was hauled off me and the man was reaching out a hand to pull my stunned self to my feet. I leant against his arm while I recovered myself and when I was able, I stood on my own. Somehow the monk was still alive, perhaps the thickness of his blood meant it bled out slower. Anyhow it was emitting a spitting, choking sound as the man leant down and held the tip of the sword to the monk's throat.

"Any last words?"

A wet laugh escaped his lips as it stared hard at us, eyes glinting in sunken sockets.

"You cannot stop the Harbinger. The Mother's ritual has begun and soon all will bask in the red rain."

If he was about to say more, I did not know for I looked away as, with a look of disgust, the man pushed the sword into the monk again. When his ragged breathing had stopped, I looked around. The man was cleaning his sword with a scrap of cloth and nodded at me as he caught my gaze.

"My thanks there, you saved me. I believe introductions are in order. I am Vaas."

"I am Inior," I replied, "do you really know how to get us out of here?"

Vaas sighed and gestured with his sword towards the body of the monk.

"Unfortunately, I believe that thing has given us our answer. Unless I stop whatever it is this 'Mother' of theirs is doing, I fear we shall all be lost. Of course, I will not force one such as yourself to accompany me on so dangerous a task, but I fear that you would simply fall victim to another of this Covenant were I to let you go your own way."

I felt something new swell in my chest. For a second, I was reminded of stories from my earlier childhood, of knights and heroes who would battle impossible odds to save the day. In

Vaas I felt I had found such a hero.

"I'll come with you," I said without hesitation. He looked at me hard for a second then nodded.

"Very well. Whatever you did to distract that monk may yet come in useful again but when the fighting starts stay behind me." I nodded and followed swiftly after as he began to walk to the door.

~

The next few hours, or was it days, were spent in a whirl of adrenaline and awe. We found our way back to halls that were filled with light and decoration, and it was there that I saw Vaas unleashed. I had grown used to seeing bodies by now, having been surrounded by the dead for the majority of my time here but the ferocity and speed at which Vaas cut down any monks that crossed his path made me truly believe that we could take on this entire mountain's worth at once. As he charged, Vaas bellowed a warcry in a language I didn't understand, save for a single word that I knew to be the name of a distant kingdom, and his spinning sword sent robed figures tumbling to the ground with each stroke and there was nowhere else in the world I wanted to be but watch him do his work.

We continued upwards as much as we could until eventually, we came to a great wooden door that barred our path. Its guards dispatched, Vaas barged against it and slowly it swung open. The first thing that struck me in the room beyond was the sunlight streaming in though a large window and I realised that we must have made our way to the top of the mountain. The sunlight seemed like such a strange thing to me now that I was completely distracted from what was happening in the rest of the room.

The sudden burst of pressure, followed by the sound of shattering glass, brought me back to reality and I saw Vaas flying backwards through a sheet of stained glass ahead of me. He must have run heroically forward to attack the figures I now saw on the far side of the room. All of them were bedecked in the red robes of the Covenant, their bodies completely hidden by crimson folds until they looked less like people and more like piles of cloth. They were positioned in a loose circle around one in the center who was standing, clawed hand outstretched.

I looked to Vaas and he was lying still; I could see glass shards surrounding him, some looked to have pierced his armor and flesh. My breath caught in my throat as I realised my heroic guardian, who had cut his way through what felt like the entire monastery to stop what was happening here, wasn't going to get up again.

"Come, child," whispered the Reverend Mother from the center of the circle, "come, as I have foreseen and give us the blood of power needed to bring forth the Harbinger and the age of the red rain." I felt that tug then, the same tug I had felt earlier, that pulled on my veins, inside my blood itself to drive me forward. I took a step, then another and the Reverend Mother slid from inside her ropes a wicked looking knife whose deep scarlet blade glinted in the streaming sun. She held it out before her as the surrounding monks began to chant rhythmically as she threw back her hood revealing a true nightmare. It was her eyes that I saw first, or rather her lack of them, for dark portals of twisting crimson sat where they should be in a face that writhed and moved as though worms were crawling underneath her skin. She opened her mouth and I heard the voice inside my head repeat her summons for me to approach yet nothing came from behind her waving, leech like tongue save a tide of thick, black liquid. I wanted to run, my body screamed at me to, but I could not fight her will driving me on towards her and the waiting blade.

A rent appeared in the room as though someone had slid a knife through the fabric of the world and a dark light began to spill from, twisting like smoke as it rose to the ceiling.

"He comes, the Harbinger is called, hungering for a taste of the blood of power." Her voice whispered inside my head as I entered the circle of worshipers who were still chanting beneath their hoods. I tried one final time to pull away as the Reverend Mother raised herself before me, raising the knife high. Her voice bellowed in my head.

"Let this final sacrifice, a final spilling of blood of power, sustain you, Harbinger of the red rain, and bind you to my will." As she uttered these words, I felt her power holding me shift as though it were being directed elsewhere. Without thinking I felt my own power surge through me, as I channeled all my fear and anger into a leap that caught hold of her face and neck with my hands.

Her skin gave way and tore easily as though it were made of wet parchment, and I felt my hands suddenly become slick with more of the viscous liquid that flowed from beneath her torn skin. My powers went to work quickly, channeling as much of my bound-up rage as I could and soon, she staggered, the soft, rotten bones of her face giving way beneath my fingers and, at her neck my power decimated her flesh until, with a final crack, her head toppled free from her body.

I staggered back becoming aware that the chanting from around me had not stopped, in fact, it seemed to have only increased in fervor and volume. It was then I saw the rent in the world widen. Something was coming through, pushing aside the dark light that flowed from it, I saw a blinding white wisp of what could be a hand, then an arm and maybe even a head. I began to back away; I had expected the ritual to stop once the Reverend Mother was dealt with. Maybe I could have then attended to Vaas, told him I had completed our quest and that we could both escape. But the thing was now halfway through the tear.

I was turning to run when, in fraction of a second, it seemed to flicker from the rent and collided full force with myself. I was pushed down to one knee by the weight of it latching on and I felt a presence blossom inside my head. This was not like the Reverend Mother's voice had felt, this felt alive as it squirmed around inside my mind and fully assimilated into my body. For a second, I felt its thoughts as they subsumed my own, what it wanted to do, no what it would do to the world now it had a had a body. I felt that it called itself Olgirath but the Covenant knew it as something else, The Harbinger. And then, I felt nothing.

~

Olgirath allowed the boy's memories to flash through his mind as the last of his soul was torn away and devoured. He savored every last drop of the fear and pain this body had felt as it relived them in its final moments. As the last of what had been Inior faded away, Olgirath pulled himself to his feet and a smile split the lips of his new face. He took a step forward and bright spectral wings burst from his back causing the red robed figures surrounding him, who had started to make their way towards him, to fall to their knees, their heads bowed.

"The Harbinger of the Red Rain is here," cried one and the rest started chanting in low rhythmic voices.

"Praise him. Praise him."

The stench of devotion, of blind obedience coming off them was overpowering to Olgirath and it disgusted him. He raised his hand and felt the tingle of his immense power flow through now able to be directed by a physical body. Without even a cry the figures around him burst into dust and were scattered on the breeze that drifted through the tower.

Olgirath shifted, his power running rampant through the child's body and molding it to better suit his wishes. Bones cracked and flesh split as he grew taller, hooves bursting from the wraps around what had been his feet and layers of scales pushing through warping skin. When he felt the crown of horns push their way through his skull, he knew the change was complete and paused by one of the mirrors to admire his new form. Any last semblance of the boy Inior was gone replaced in its entirety by the spirit of Olgirath given flesh.

"Defiler, Demon, I curse you."

The voice was weak and croaking yet still with a trace of defiance. It was coming from a man lying in a slowly growing pool of blood from the numerous shards of glass that pierced his body. Yet, despite his encroaching death, he still held a sword tightly in his hand and was staring up at Olgirath with an intense hatred in his eyes.

Delving again into Inior's memories Olgirath remembered this man. Inior had known him as Vaas and they'd faced the horrors of this place together.

"Oh, Vaas, how far you've fallen." His voice was a low whisper of overlapping voices and he saw a flicker of fear flash across Vaas' eyes as he heard his name. "You know Inior looked up to you, Vaas, in the short while you were together. You were the one thing in this place that he felt kept him safe and now look at you. Couldn't even do that, could you."

He smiled with a mouth full of needle like teeth as Vaas looked away and tried in vain to push himself to his feet, but his legs gave out under him.

"You're pathetic," he hissed, some of the voices now screaming, some sobbing through his whispers.

With a flick of his head, he turned away and heard the wet smack behind him as his power slammed Vaas' head off the stone floor. Almost as an afterthought, Olgirath reached out and ensnared the man's life essence as it tried to slip away and pulled it within his body to feed on at his leisure. Then he made his way over to the window and looked out over the land stretching away far below the cliff. The smoke from a village curled its way into the air not far from the base of the cliff and he could sense its inhabitants on the currents of power from here. They would be the first to truly bear witness to his rebirth in this world. He raised his clawed hands, and the first blood red drops of rain began to fall.

ARIANRHOD

ALYS HALL

Alys Hall is a writer and poet from North Wales. Her writing seeks to give space to environmental concerns, marginalised voices from the LGBTQ+ community and Welsh myth. She has previously been published by the Welsh women's magazine Codi Pais and, most recently, in Sonder: An Anthology alongside her peers on the MA Creative Writing course at Bangor University. You can follow her on @alys.catrin

I'r merched sy'n mynnu eu rhyddid.
To the women who insist on their freedom

This story is a modern retelling of the original Mabinogi tales.

"KING MATH – HERE I PRESENT TO YOU THE FAIREST, MOST beautiful woman to walk this land – Arianrhod, daughter of Dôn," Gwydion said.

Arianrhod stepped forward, gleaming, and bowed to Math, King of Gwynedd. She kept her eyes trained to the floor until he bade her to rise. Her head swam from the red carpet beneath her feet. She listened to them talking and felt her back straining from her exaggerated bow.

This was no average ceremony. The women who stood in line behind her claimed they were the fairest and most beautiful in all Cymru. Courtiers and guests mingled with royalty and the hall bustled with people who were laughing and drinking. Up until the ceremony, King Math snapped at the waiting staff who tripped over their own feet to bring him refreshments and any smatterings of gossip that circulated the hall.

Goewin, the King's former footholder, sat in the corner of the room in shame. Her body shook whenever she heard the King yell at his waiting staff. Her head drooped and she let the hot tears flow down her face. Only virgins could act as the King's footholder and she was now stripped of the position.

Goewin wrung her dress between her hands and blew her nose on her sodden handkerchief. Nobody stood there to comfort her and so she let out a torrent of emotions for all to see. When one of her sobs became audible to the guests, the King ordered that a maid take her away from the hall at once.

Arianrhod glanced at Goewin's sagging body and wondered what future lay ahead for her. The King needed a new footholder as Goewin had been raped by one of his horsemen. She would surely be forced to marry the man and even find herself banished from the court. Arianrhod's stomach clenched with the thought. She would have done anything to avoid such a fate. It would have brought shame on her and severed the alliance her family had with the court. They enjoyed the riches of the King's castle and Arianrhod could imagine living out her days here. It was the reason she chose to stand in line with the other women.

All the women who preceded Arianrhod were taken away. One was dragged away crying and screaming as the King surveyed the next in line. Arianrhod, being the last, tried to distract herself from the sounds of crying and the King's admonishments.

"Not thin enough."

"She isn't pleasing to look at."

"Not dainty in the slightest."

Each admonishment sent a blow to the women and Arianrhod tried not to fear. She surveyed the hall in all its glory and thought about how being a footholder in this grand castle would secure her future. She looked up at the jewelled seats and imagined herself at the King of Gwynedd's feet with enough riches to last a lifetime. Gowns would be made ready for her, and food would never be scarce.

The women who preceded Arianrhod walked away, disgraced, with their hearts heavy from a single sweep of Math's hand. Arianrhod took a brief look over to her brother Gwydion, the King's magician, for reassurance. Her brother stood on the King's right-hand side and had so far made the announcements for each woman's birth and their credentials. Arianrhod smiled at Gwydion and he winked at her discreetly. She would be the next footholder, and with her brother's help she would secure the position for the rest of her days. And now, here she was, bowing before the King. It was her turn to glow.

"Yes, she is beautiful indeed, and fair. A gem to your family name, Gwydion. You have been a loyal magician, and your sister would be a loyal footholder to me," King Math of Gwynedd said. "However, I cannot simply accept her as such. To be my footholder, she must be pure of heart and body. Have you, fair lady, been pure?"

"Yes, my King," Arianrhod said.

"Gwydion, take out the rod," King Math said. "And rise, fair lady, so that I may see you in the light."

Arianrhod rose from her bow and the King nodded in approval. Gwydion waved his fingertips in the air and a silver rod appeared on the floor before her, glimmering beneath the candlelight. Gwydion enchanted it and Arianrhod watched the rod slither along the carpet.

"Step over the rod. It will test your purity," said the King.

Arianrhod stood tall with all the eyes of the hall on her. She inhaled deeply and lifted her foot. Her family, friends, loyal maidens, and guests watched in anticipation as she started to step foot across the silver rod. One foot landed on the other side and she exhaled. Arianrhod, determined now to pass the test, brought her other foot to join it.

For a split second, she thought she had succeeded. She readied herself to turn around and smile at her brother and the King. But, like an ocean wave crashing over her, she felt her body flood with sweat. A stabbing pain shot through her stomach and she squeezed her eyes shut.

Two slithering creatures poured onto the carpet and Arianrhod fell, reeling with shock. The hall gasped as the two beings emerged from the folds of her white dress. They slithered down her thighs and onto the floor in two balls of flesh. One was blue, resembling a sea monster, and the other looked like a human baby enveloped in a transparent ball. The guests stepped away, widening the circle around Arianrhod. The King recoiled in disgust when he saw the creatures pooling on the floor.

Arianrhod screamed in horror. All the other sounds of the hall were drowned by the gut-wrenching scream that tore through her body. She lifted her head blearily, catching sight of the blue beast crawling across the floor. How had something so beast-like emerged from her body? Arianrhod later heard it had been thrown into the sea and lived as a spirit of the waters. She stared at the human baby that lay in a heap of fluid on the floor.

It did not move nor make a sound, likely dead at birth.

Arianrhod looked up at Gwydion. He gazed down at her in disgust and refused to even hold out a hand to help her. Rage gripped her and she pointed her finger at him.

"This is your fault! You did this," she yelled for all the hall to hear. "My own brother."

Gwydion turned his head and beckoned the servants. Arianrhod screamed again and she was dragged away by multiple hands. Grief welled inside her for all that had occurred in those brief few moments. She watched the hall vanish from her eyes, all the candlelights, laughter and joy. She sobbed and sobbed, unable to stop the flood of tears from escaping her. Shame bubbled inside her gut and she felt the numbness set in.

Gwydion watched as his sister was pulled away. The entire hall was in uproar and the human baby on the floor was forgotten, something discarded carelessly on the ground. The King waved his hands at some of his servants and ordered them to find more virgins immediately. He would surely take any who could step over the rod.

Gwydion approached the baby on the floor and realised quickly that it was a boy. Gwydion lifted him, oozing with liquid, and felt his blood pumping, alive, on his fingertips. He took the baby boy away from the hall and carried him to his private rooms. Gwydion set him down on a table and plied open the folds of liquid that enveloped him. In one burst, when the air reached him, the boy started to cry.

Gwydion opened a chest in his rooms and enchanted it to let the boy rest inside. Once Arianrhod was banished, he would raise the boy in the court and find a use for him.

~

Arianrhod, banished from the King of Gwynedd's court, came to live on a remote fortress on the sea. The fortress, surrounded by black rocks, was west of Llandwrog and far enough away from the court. It was now called Caer Arianrhod. She lived with a couple of maids on the caer and Gwydion enchanted it to prevent her from leaving the desolate island.

Despairing for her future, Arianrhod felt that she would wither away on this remote place and die. She'd considered hauling herself out of the castle and onto the rocks for a swift end but felt the need for revenge burning. She would live to one day slight the King and her so-called brother. If she lived, there was hope.

A few months after she'd been banished from the court, Gwydion sent his sister a visitor. Arianrhod watched from the caer as a familiar figure came out of the boat and walked between her two maids. She saw the familiar brown braids hanging down to her waist and her careful walk up to the entryway. Arianrhod ran to the door and opened it, welcoming in the guest with open arms. The visitor who came on the boat was none other than Goewin.

"Why did Gwydion send you here?" Arianrhod asked.

"Gwydion didn't send me - I wanted to come here," Goewin said. "I asked him if I could come and he relented."

Arianrhod, feeling a certain kinship with this fallen woman, welcomed her in and they cried together as the sea wind hammered against the fortress walls. They embraced and confided in one another about their exile. Fearing for her life, Goewin asked to stay with Arianrhod in her fortress. The man who raped her was married to another woman and therefore Goewin was destitute. She was allowed to stay and Arianrhod felt hope kindle in their newfound friendship.

The sky burned red from the sun that set over them that night. They vowed to always protect and support one another, no matter what challenges came to face them. The sea battered against the rocks and the wind roared through the caer's windows. They promised that they would weather the storm together and find happiness in their exile.

Goewin spent her days knitting until her fingers reddened and Arianrhod read book after book until her eyes burned. At the end of each day, the women watched the waves outside of the caer and pointed at the boats and seagulls. Arianrhod hoped that her son, the sea creature, was faring well in these waters. She thought about him each time she looked out onto the waves.

They knew the sea by now and the way it danced, and even raged. When the waters were still and the wind quiet, they would venture out onto the rocks and skim stones that rippled the surface. They laughed and sang with the maids, capturing what glimmers of joy they could in their exile. When they argued, they brought the sea to shame with their roaring, until they forgave one another and brought peace to the caer.

Over time, Goewin and Arianrhod came to be lovers. Their friendship blossomed into a deep love for one another. The love they shared grew with every passing day and they yearned to spend every waking moment in each other's presence. Arianrhod and Goewin lived and breathed for each other and felt that it was only natural to share a room and sleep together. They met each morning and closed each day together in their rooms.

The women made the caer their home. Goewin and the maids would bring supplies from the village of Llandwrog once a week and the odd book or trinket. A man on a boat would arrive, every Friday, to take them to the land to restock. Arianrhod, from Gwydion's curse, forgot what the land felt like, what the trees were and how they changed. She remembered the land from how the women spoke about it.

Arianrhod could see the coast of Dinas Dinlle in the distance and, every so often, she could make out figures on the beach. She forgot what different faces looked like. She grew so accustomed to Goewin, the maids and the boat man that she believed they were the only people left on the face of the earth. Arianrhod knew the ocean waves and the roar of the wind better than she knew the people that walked on the land.

~

Gwydion, without Arianrhod's knowledge, raised the son she had birthed in the court. He grew over the years and dove headlong into boyhood. Gwydion took his nephew under his wing and taught him most of what he knew, besides his precious magical abilities. The boy was skilled at crafting, building and especially accurate when he threw stones at targets. His eye was sharper than any that Gwydion had ever known.

"Well done, young boy. You are improving every day," Gwydion said on the eve of his eighth birthday. "It is about time that you were given a name, but it cannot be from me."

"Who, uncle, will give me a name?" The boy asked.

"Your mother, Arianrhod. You will meet her and she will name you."

"Can you not name me, uncle? Must it be my mother?"

"No, my boy, I cannot name you," Gwydion replied. "It is tradition that the first words uttered to you by your mother shall be your name."

Arianrhod received word from her brother that, after eight years on the caer, she would be granted her freedom from exile. She felt a lightness in her step after Gwydion lifted the enchantment and felt a yearning to see and feel the land again. For years, she had been a part of the sea, but she was no sea creature. She yearned to feel the earth beneath her feet again and touch the barks of the trees. She missed her family dearly, but she knew there was no way of returning to them again, even after so much time.

On the day of her release, Arianrhod prepared to leave the caer. Goewin helped her onto the old boat and the boat man rowed them to the shore. Arianrhod watched the land coming closer and closer to her, as though it came to meet her on arrival. Goewin held her hand and kissed her forehead.

"Paid a bod ofn, Arianrhod. Don't be afraid. The land welcomes you home," Goewin said.

Arianrhod closed her eyes and felt the sea wind caress her face. The wind whispered in her ear and she felt the land draw nearer. When the boat reached the shore, Goewin helped Arianrhod onto the soft sand. She collapsed to her knees and buried her face to the ground. She gathered sand in her hands and balled them into fists. Goewin knelt beside her and, after a time, led her towards the dunes. The grass of the dunes swayed in the distance with the force of the wind, as though they beckoned her onward. Arianrhod walked through the fine sand and relished in the feel of the speckles that stuck between her fingers. She ran her fingers through the dune grass and walked out of the sand. The earth hardened beneath her feet and she knelt to touch the ground.

Arianrhod's face, wet with tears, broke into a smile. She took away her boots and felt the grass kiss the soles of her feet. Arianrhod ran, laughing, and Goewin struggled to catch up with her. Her dress flew around her in the wind and she waved her arms at Goewin from a distance. Arianrhod, in those brief moments, fell in love with the land again.

A week after her release, Gwydion sent word to his sister about a meeting. He had arranged for her, Goewin and the maids to live in a small house in the woods, not far from Llandwrog. Arianrhod agreed, reluctantly, to meet with her brother. She sent him two words, by hand, for him to read in advance: "No tricks." She knew she needed to be on her guard. Her brother, versed in the magical arts, could deceive her with a simple wave of his hand.

Gwydion knocked on the door of the house with his nephew at his side. The boy trembled and rubbed his hands together. He knew the court's tales about his mother and feared that she might curse him on the spot. He held his uncle's gaze and wanted desperately to be protected by his magic. They crossed the threshold of the house and met the two women and the maids who sat by the table. Gwydion took in the sight of these fallen women gathered in the house and tried not to sneer. He noted that Goewin hadn't lost her beauty, nor had his sister.

Arianrhod rose and greeted Gwydion. Eight years had passed and nothing much had changed about him. He still wore the same white tunic and brushed his fair locks behind his head. Arianrhod noted the boy's presence and nodded to him. The boy, frozen on the spot, stared at his mother in awe. Arianrhod's eyes narrowed when she saw his lip tremble.

"Gwydion, who is this boy? An apprentice magician?" Arianrhod asked.

"No, Arianrhod. This is your son, born eight years ago in the King's court," Gwydion said.

Arianrhod gripped onto a nearby chair for support. She felt tears swell in her eyes as she took in the young boy in front of her. She remembered the fateful day in a sudden wave and her chest heaved with the same sob that gripped her. Her eyes flickered to Gwydion, who watched her every reaction dispassionately. Arianrhod's heart ached before it raged. No tricks, she'd asked. No tricks.

"You kept him from me after all of this time?" Arianrhod said.

"And now he is here. He needs a name, sister," Gwydion replied. "You are his mother."

"I thought he was dead."

Arianrhod's face crumbled and she looked away from the boy. The shame she had endured on that day came back to her. The embarrassment and disgrace returned, melding the years that separated them. What was worse was how Gwydion had hidden her son to use him against her and remind her of the humiliation all those years ago.

"A name, Arianrhod," Gwydion insisted.

"The boy will never have a name unless it is given to him by me," Arianrhod snapped. The tynged, the fate was set in place and Gwydion felt the power of her words shake the house.

Gwydion dug his heels into the floor. This was not how he had expected her to react. The boy stood, dumb and motionless, watching the exchange. Gwydion bit his lip and inclined his head. His head ran away with him as he started concocting a plan that would put an end to this foolish fate.

"So be it. Your son shall be nameless," Gwydion said. He turned on his heel and took the boy with him. Arianrhod kept her head turned away and felt the tears burning her cheeks. When they left, she walked to the window and watched her son disappear.

~

Months passed and Gwydion set about his plan. His nephew didn't know about the finer details but knew that it would involve tricking his mother. The boy remembered the look on his mother's face when he realised who he was. It was etched in his memories, haunting his dreams. He didn't want to trick her, but he had no power to change his uncle's mind. When Gwydion decided on something, it would be so.

The boy went over the plan with his uncle. He practiced his stone throwing and tried not to think about how his mother would react. He felt angry for how his mother gave him this fate but felt equally angry that his uncle would continue to treat her so. He agreed to carry out the plan and Gwydion sent the boy to the woods where Arianrhod lived.

After her tynged, Gwydion enchanted the woods to cage Arianrhod from the outside world. She spent her days reading or walking with her lover Goewin. After watching her movements, Gwydion timed the encounter with the boy to perfection. He knew that Arianrhod and Goewin would walk the same path in the woods at that exact point in time. Gwydion hid behind one of the bushes and peered through the leaves. The boy stood, stones dangling from his pockets, to wait for the women to appear on the path.

Walking along the beaten path, Arianrhod and Goewin chattered away. They pointed out certain birds to each other or identified the different species of tree that surrounded them. They often walked barefoot together, revelling in the feel of the earth on their feet. Arianrhod spotted a fair-haired boy playing with stones in the distance. His back was turned away from them and so Arianrhod called to him. The boy, keeping to Gwydion's plan, refused to turn. He threw a stone towards one of the wrens and hit one square on the chest. The wren squawked and flew away in a fit of anger.

"Incredible! The fair-haired one with a skillful hand," Arianrhod clapped. Goewin, on the other hand, scowled at the boy for disturbing the wrens.

From where he had been hiding in the bush, Gwydion jumped out in victory and lifted the boy in his arms. Arianrhod froze beside Goewin and watched her brother pounce on the young boy.

"And he is named! Lleu Llaw Gyffes - the fair-haired one with the skillful hand," Gwydion laughed, but the boy was not laughing with him.

Arianrhod buried her face in her hands and Goewin held her shoulders. Her shoulders shook beneath Goewin's hands and she felt the pain of seeing Gwydion wreak havoc on her body. Arianrhod felt the heat of her crying scald her skin and she held onto Goewin to keep herself upright.

"How dare you?" Goewin said to Gwydion. "You and your wretched tricks —"

"Your son is named. Next, he will take up arms and he will soon become a man," Gwydion cheered.

"That boy will never possess arms unless I arm him," Arianrhod yelled in fury.

Gwydion set Lleu down on his feet. The second tynged settled in the air around them. The woods shivered from Arianrhod's words, and the wrens nestled closer together overhead. The magic rippled along her fingertips and she clenched her hands into fists.

Enraged, Gwydion wrapped his cloak around Lleu and they vanished out of sight. Arianrhod mourned for the loss of her son and how her brother continued to use him against her. Goewin led her sobbing body away from the scene and consoled her. She would hold her in the bed they shared and take the flood of tears that came. Arianrhod would wonder whether her brother held her son under some spell. He used him to manipulate her and she dreaded to think what her brother would do next.

Bound to the woods by his spell, Arianrhod was powerless to stop him. She would have done anything to have retrieved her son from him. Goewin and the maids would send word or try to find Gwydion themselves, but it came to no avail. He escaped their searching and Lleu Llaw Gyffes was under the King's protection. Unless he went himself to Arianrhod's woods, her son was lost to her and Gwydion would continue to pour lies down his throat.

~

It took years for Gwydion to hatch his next plan. Lleu Llaw Gyffes grew into a young man and became renowned for his skills and horsemanship. Gwydion despaired that his nephew would be deprived of weapons because of his sister's tynged. He rejoiced that he was given a name but felt angered that he could not use the weapons that he sorely deserved. Lleu watched as his friends took arms and his mother's tynged stopped him from joining them. Gwydion evaded Goewin's prying into his affairs and ensured Lleu's protection by the Crown. If it took years to arm him, so be it.

Gwydion told Lleu that he would be able to see his mother again. They would need to disguise themselves as bards and visit Arianrhod to ask for lodgings for the night. Lleu listened to his uncle's plan and felt his gut twisting with the memories of his mother. He remembered the tricks they had played on his mother when he was a young boy and he regretted them sorely. For the first time, Lleu put his foot down with his uncle.

"No more tricks," Lleu said to him.

"Don't you want to see your mother again, after so long? Yes, she may have rejected you, but haven't you wondered how she is, what she looks like?" Gwydion said.

Lleu admitted that he had done little else when he thought of her. There wasn't a day that went by when he didn't wonder about his mother Arianrhod. He went as far as to wonder whether she was wondering about him. Gwydion insisted that Arianrhod cared little for him, but from her reactions to his arrival at the cottage, he couldn't have been sure. Gwydion wouldn't allow him to see her alone, nor did Lleu have any idea on how to find her if he wanted to. His only link to his mother was through Gwydion.

"In order to see her, I must disguise myself as a bard?" Lleu asked.

"Precisely. We must act the part and, after spending the night, we will return here. She will be none the wiser," Gwydion asked.

"So, it is a trick," Lleu said.

"She will know nothing of it. I will not taunt her any longer – it is child's play," Gwydion assured him. "You will see her and she will remain unharmed. I know how you care for her. She is your mother and it is natural that you feel this way."

Lleu relented to his uncle's pleas and agreed to disguise himself as a bard with him. Gwydion used his magic to make their disguises as convincing as possible. Lleu felt the familiar feeling from his boyhood of something not being right. He trusted his uncle from his boyhood and that was precisely what made him fear the worst.

Gwydion transported them by his cloak to the woods where Arianrhod lived with Goewin and the maids. Lleu looked around and noticed that not much besides the seasons had changed since he was last there as a young boy. Gwydion led the way along the footpath and Lleu followed closely behind. The same childish fears gripped him as a man just as they did when he was young. He resisted the urge to hold his uncle's hand like he did as a boy.

The house stood in the same spot as it had done all those years ago. The disguise felt heavy on his body and he wanted to see his mother as Lleu, not a bard. Never had this hiraeth, this longing to return to this place felt more potent. Gwydion knocked his hand on the door and Lleu held his breath. Curiosity would always get the better of him, in the end.

Goewin answered the door. She had aged since their last visit, but almost imperceptibly. Her eyes flickered from one bard to the other and she beckoned for Arianrhod to come. A maid set down her dough of bread and held onto a kitchen knife. They could have been thieves for all they knew.

"Who is it, Goewin?" Arianrhod asked.

"We are lost here in these woods. We are bards from Môn searching for lodgings. Would you be so kind as to accommodate us for the night?" Gwydion said.

Not only had Gwydion changed their appearances, but their voices too. Lleu tried not to stare openly at his mother, who stood behind Goewin. Unlike Goewin, age showed itself on her face openly. There were faint lines across her forehead and dark circles underneath her eyes. She seemed much thinner than the last time.

Before Goewin spoke, Arianrhod opened the door wider and let the two bards inside. The maid placed the knife down and carried on kneading the dough on the countertop. Gwydion, prepared for the role, started to recite some verses and he gesticulated his hands as he spoke. Goewin laughed and urged him to carry on.

"What of the other bard?" Arianrhod asked.

"He is being trained in the arts. He will recite some lines tonight - I assure you," Gwydion said, patting his hand on Lleu's shoulder.

The sky darkened outside and Gwydion opened his satchel. He took out a couple of bottles of mead and set them down on the table. Goewin clapped her hands, overjoyed. Arianrhod raised her eyebrow at the bard.

"You are in no shortage of drink," Arianrhod said.

"What can I say? We are bards," Gwydion chuckled.

They settled into each other's company and laughed together into the night. Gwydion urged Lleu to recite a few lines and the women clapped when he recited some poetry he learned from his schooling. When they all made their way to bed, Gwydion was alert. Lleu lay down and watched his uncle pace in circles. He stared at the ceiling and felt tears threaten to fall down his cheeks. To have seen his mother had moved him more than he dared to admit.

"Do not hold this against me, Lleu," Gwydion said.

"What?"

Gwydion turned around. He extended out his arms and his palms faced the window. Lleu watched, mouth agape, as his uncle murmured his spells. In the distance, Lleu could hear horses galloping towards the house. Lleu jumped out of his bed and grabbed Gwydion with both hands.

"What have you done? You said no tricks. A disguise and no more," Lleu snapped.

Before Lleu could say more, he could hear the women outside of the bedroom. Arianrhod threw the door open and tugged Lleu and Gwydion out.

"Hurry! Hurry! We are under attack! Arm yourselves!" Arianrhod yelled.

Arianrhod opened a chest and hauled out a couple of swords and shields. She handed Lleu a sword and shield as she dug around the cupboard for more. Gwydion, unable to believe his luck, laughed and raised his arms into the sky. The sound of galloping stopped and Arianrhod stopped too. She had heard that laughter before, long ago. She turned her head and saw Gwydion and Lleu, without their disguises, standing before her.

"You armed him! Now Lleu is a man. Soon, he will marry and have children. Your evil fates will plight him no more," Gwydion roared in victory.

Arianrhod looked at Lleu who held the sword and shield in his two hands. Her eyes flickered to his face and she took in how much her son had grown. He was indeed becoming a man, and it terrified her.

"Mother, I never –" Lleu started.

"Lleu Llaw Gyffes will never have a wife made of flesh," Arianrhod said.

Gwydion could have killed his sister at once. Lleu's eyes widened as the tynged escaped her lips. Goewin and the maids ran inside and staggered in shock to see Gwydion and Lleu. They now understood why the attack had suddenly ceased.

"You would deprive your son of a wife?" Gwydion raged at her. "You selfish, inconsiderate witch. I should kill you now, with my bare hands –"

"Uncle, it is done," Lleu pulled his uncle away from Arianrhod.

"We are nowhere near done. Mark my words, Arianrhod – you have not succeeded. This boy will have his wife even if it kills me. And I will spare your life now so you may see it."

"Get out!" Goewin yelled.

"With pleasure," Gwydion spat. "And do not think that I am ignorant to your relationship. It is immoral and disgusting."

Gwydion grabbed Lleu's shoulder and they vanished into thin air. Arianrhod didn't have the will to cry. She stared at the spot where her brother and son stood some mere seconds ago. Goewin ran to her and tried to console her. Arianrhod couldn't feel nor hear Goewin in those moments. Severed from reality, she could only see her son's face in front of her. Arianrhod fell to her knees and touched the place where he stood. She then breathed in the same air he once breathed.

~

Gwydion and Lleu landed back in the King's Hall. Lleu fell back onto the ground from the impact and Gwydion stormed over to the King's throne. Lleu chased his uncle and recognised the feeling from how he resented Arianrhod for the tynged. His body shook with rage from his mother's tynged and his face burned with the embarrassment of having trusted his uncle so fully. All the pent-up emotions began to surge through his chest. His hands and arms were shaking and his palms were coated with his own sweat. Gwydion flicked his hand and Lleu felt himself pushed back onto the floor. He staggered from the spell and felt his back thud on the floor. Lleu hauled himself up again and continued to tail his uncle.

"Uncle! Stop this nonsense at once," Lleu snapped.

"I know you are angry, Lleu, but believe you me – there is nobody in Cymru angrier than I am now," Gwydion shouted from the King's Hall.

King Math of Gwynedd heard Gwydion before he saw him. Gwydion kicked open the King's doors and didn't even so much as bow to the King and the virgin footholder. He waved his arms around and explained what had just occurred with his sister Arianrhod. The King listened and became infuriated himself that Arianrhod placed another tynged on the boy. When he heard the nature of the tynged, he frowned and understood Gwydion's rage. Lleu watched the exchange from afar, powerless to intervene.

"Arianrhod is indeed cruel, Gwydion. But do not despair – I have an idea. You said the tynged means that Lleu cannot have a wife made of flesh. Well then, you must fashion a wife for him made from the earth," The King said.

Gwydion admitted that he liked this idea. Lleu walked forward to speak, but Gwydion told him to stay silent for now. The virgin footholder tried not to sigh or even roll her eyes as the men bickered. The King insisted that it would be simple.

"My King, if it is within your power to have the materials gathered – oak, broom and meadowsweet preferably – then I may be able to fashion him a wife out of flowers," Gwydion said.

"It is done. My loyal servants will collect the materials that you need and the boy will have a wife," The King said.

The servants went ahead to collect the oak, broom and meadowsweet at once. It took a day for them to collect the quantities that would satisfy Gwydion, but it was done. The servants, sweating from the exertion, retreated to the kitchens after Gwydion took the buckets from them. He set down the three materials in the King's Hall and Lleu felt the familiar feeling of discomfort enter his stomach. The King grinned when he saw the excitement on his magician's face.

"We will make her now. There is no time to lose!" Gwydion laughed.

Lleu, who now stood by the King's throne, watched his uncle summoning the elements. Gwydion knelt onto the red carpet and raised his arms above his head. Lleu, the King and the footholder could only hear the mumblings and grumblings of a madman at his work. Slowly, the oak, broom and meadowsweet rose from the buckets and came together. They blended in front of Gwydion and started to take shape.

The King gripped the arms of his throne and Lleu closed his eyes from the light that came from the scene. When he opened them again, there was a lady standing in the centre of the hall. She looked like any other lady, besides the abundance of flowers in her hair and across her dress.

"Here she is. Blodeuwedd, a lady made from flowers," Gwydion said.

The footholder almost fainted at the sight. The King's mouth lay open and Lleu held his breath, waiting to see what she would do. She stared at Gwydion and he held out his hand to her. Blodeuwedd took his hand and he led her to Lleu.

"Can she... speak?" Lleu asked his uncle.

"Yes. Here, Blodeuwedd – here is Lleu Llaw Gyffes. He will be your husband."

"Hello, Lleu Llaw Gyffes," Blodeuwedd said.

~

Word reached Arianrhod about Blodeuwedd's creation. Arianrhod was enraged that Gwydion and the King would go as far as to create a wife out of the ground for her son. She felt enraged at herself for having uttered the words in the first place. To have punished her son for the crimes of Gwydion and the King was a mistake. Lleu didn't deserve to suffer because of Gwydion's tricks.

Nobody was angrier at Arianrhod than herself. She felt infuriated that these men had brought out this terrifying darkness within her. Gwydion would not get the better of her now. The men who had slighted, abused, and shunned her would not succeed again.

~

Miles and miles away, Lleu Llaw Gyffes came to know Blodeuwedd. She was quiet and reserved most of the time, besides when they spoke about the flowers in the King's meadows. She piped up and talked about the various species that graced their fields during Spring. Blodeuwedd listened to Lleu when he spoke about his weapons, armory, and horses, but found that she didn't find much interest in him at all. She started to feel duped by creation for having been made to be his wife. She sensed that he didn't regard her with much interest either. They were worlds apart, but Gwydion insisted that they would marry soon.

Lleu wondered whether the union to Blodeuwedd could be stopped. Neither Lleu nor Blodeuwedd wanted the marriage to go ahead and Gwydion was blind to it. Lleu also wondered whether his mother and another tynged could stop it from happening. When Lleu told Gwydion how things stood with Blodeuwedd, he refused to listen.

"What? She is exquisite. She is beautiful – one of the most beautiful women to have graced this earth. What more do you want from a wife?" Gwydion said to him.

"She is wonderful, yes, but I don't think I can marry her," Lleu said.

"You will marry her. I will not pluck another woman out of the earth – I might not be so lucky a second time. You cannot keep taking from the elements and expect a perfect result each time," Gwydion said. "It has been decided. Do not worry, my boy, your feelings will change in time. Once the union is sealed, you will love her dearly."

Blodeuwedd had nobody to confide in about her feelings. She would be struck by Gwydion or even the King if she were to voice her discontent. Silently, she wanted a different life. She felt as though the earth and Gwydion had cheated her out of her own existence. She had been created for Lleu and no more. Could she not live for herself? Blodeuwedd despaired that she had no choice in the matter and wanted desperately to be cut loose from this tynged.

Lleu decided that he needed to act. He wondered what would make Gwydion listen to him. Lleu made his way to the King's Hall and Gwydion eyed him suspiciously when he came in, knelt on one knee, and bowed before the three of them. He shivered and felt the palms of his hands start to sweat profusely.

"Lleu, what brings you away from your wife to be?" The King asked after he bade for Lleu to rise.

"I have a condition to set upon marrying Blodeuwedd that I would like to set to my uncle Gwydion," Lleu said.

"Name it," Gwydion said.

"You must release my mother from her bonds to the woods. She may roam free wherever she wishes."

Gwydion frowned at him. "And whyever would I want to let

that woman –"

"You told me to name my condition and I have. Release her," Lleu said.

"She is a danger to you and us all," Gwydion snapped. "The King would say as much –"

"Thank you, Gwydion, but I think differently," The King said. "Arianrhod has served her sentence. If she were released from the magical bonds, she may feel less inclined to place fates on your nephew."

Gwydion's fists were clenched. He knew that the King would have the last word and there was little else he would be able to do about it. Lleu watched his uncle running the idea through his head and hesitating. If unsuccessful, he knew he could plead with the King for his mother's release.

"Release her," Lleu insisted.

Gwydion stared into his nephew's eyes and saw that he wouldn't back down, especially when it came to this. He expected his nephew to have developed a hatred for her over the course of her life, but their separation seemed to have made the bond between mother and son even stronger.

"Very well, Lleu. I will release that pathetic woman from her bonds and you will be married to Blodeuwedd tomorrow," Gwydion said. He wrapped his green cloak around his shoulders and vanished.

~

Arianrhod felt him land in the woods. She was tending the garden and felt the energy of the nearby woods change when he landed. She made her way there, as though summoned by him, and saw him walking towards her in the distance. Arianrhod came to the threshold of where she could not cross. There was a huge barrier, invisible to the naked eye, that shimmered between her and Gwydion. She'd tried touching it years ago and it sent stabbing pains through her arm. She stood, metres away from him, and watched him rolling up his sleeves.

"I heard that you succeeded in making a wife for my son out of the earth," Arianrhod said. "Are you here to boast?"

"No, I am here to release you. It is your son's wish before

his wedding, but you are not to attend," Gwydion said. "If you meddle with the union, I will kill you and show no mercy."

Her brother's words sent a chill down Arianrhod's spine. His eyes were wide and his magic floated like daggers around him. He lifted his hands and chanted the spells that would release her. Arianrhod felt the creases on her forehead begin to loosen as Gwydion, line by line, broke her from the bonds that kept her in these woods and away from the world. She knelt to the earth and felt the bliss of freedom wash through her. It felt like touching the land again after being exiled to the sea. When Gwydion finished, she looked up at him. He stared down at her, expressionless, before disappearing.

Arianrhod walked past the threshold and breathed deeply. She felt the wind gather around her and whisper in her ear. She spent a time in the grace of this newfound freedom and greeted the trees that had been out of her reach. The wrens in the trees reminded her of her son, Lleu. She could see him as a boy with his rocks weighing down his pockets. He had asked for her release after all that she had done. In her mind's eye, he skipped in the distance and aimed his stones at the tree trunks.

Arianrhod walked home and wondered how she would see her son again before he married Blodeuwedd. As soon as she told Goewin what had happened, they decided to leave for the King's court. It would go against Gwydion's command, but the drive to see her son again overrode those fears. They travelled into the night on horseback and well into the morning. They stopped only for rest and provisions before continuing their path. They camped for the night in a wood near a lake but slept little. They nestled together for cover until the sun rose and they travelled further north to the court.

~

Preparations were being made for Blodeuwedd's wedding to Lleu. The maids were plaiting her hair and weaving all manner of flowers, leaves and branches into the plaits. Blodeuwedd sat and weaved herself a flower crown. Staring at the crown when she weaved it, she could barely look at herself in the mirror. She sat despondent in her white wedding dress and ignored the maids' comments about her beauty.

"Done!" The maid said. "You look a picture, Blodeuwedd. Lleu will be honoured to have you as his wife."

"Thank you," Blodeuwedd said. "Now, may I be left alone for a few moments? I suppose these will be some of my last minutes of peace for a while."

The maids bowed and left Blodeuwedd in her room. She stood up and paced the room in endless circles. She only stopped her pacing when she heard a noise from outside of her bedroom window. Blodeuwedd stuck her flowered head out of the window and spotted a figure scaling the wall. She staggered back and held her hand to her chest. Her breathing quickened and she held onto one of the posts of the four-poster bed to keep her upright. Blodeuwedd watched as the figure hauled themselves over the windowpane and into the room.

Arianrhod brushed herself off and looked up. Blodeuwedd froze, unable to comprehend why this woman had taken such pains to find her. She looked middle-aged, possibly widowed, and far too old to be scaling stone walls. Blodeuwedd stared at the knife that was sheathed on the belt of her dress and felt the breath in her lungs escape.

"Blodeuwedd," she said. "I am Arianrhod, Lleu's mother."

Arianrhod bowed to her before watching a look of utter shock pass over her face. Blodeuwedd, having heard about the mother's plight, ran to her with open arms and embraced her. Arianrhod held her and moments passed in this silent embrace. She felt tears soak into her shoulder from the young woman and her heart broke. Both women, who had suffered under Gwydion's hands, felt the bond of sacred sisterhood extend to one another, like an invisible thread hooking onto each of their hearts.

Blodeuwedd sent for the maids. Arianrhod stayed hidden when the maids came in and she listened to Blodeuwedd ordering for them to get Lleu to her room. The maids implored her to tell them what was wrong, but she kept the information away in the heart that kept the silent bond between her and Arianrhod.

"Lleu must come here at once. It is a very urgent matter concerning the proceedings of the wedding. It cannot be re-solved any other way," Blodeuwedd said.

Arianrhod and Blodeuwedd sat beside one another on the bed and waited for Lleu to arrive. Arianrhod's palms, coated with sweat, held onto Blodeuwedd for support. Her heart pounded in her chest and she wished that Goewin was there to comfort her.

Arianrhod stood up and Blodeuwedd went to answer the door. Lleu stepped in, confused that he had been summoned. He raised his head and thought Blodeuwedd had conjured an apparition.

Arianrhod ran to her son and flung her arms around him. She expected to see Gwydion behind him, but relaxed when she realised her son was alone. They stood in their embrace for what felt like an age and wiped each other's tears. They were silent, unable to exchange a single word to one another. Blodeuwedd watched them in silence. It took a while for Lleu to think of the words to say to her.

"I am sorry that I did not seek you out. You must understand that my uncle, your brother, made it difficult –"

"I am the one who must apologise," Arianrhod said quickly. "You must know that I regret my actions more than you could ever know."

"But why the name? Why the arms and why the wife?" Lleu asked. It was the question that had been on his mind ever since Blodeuwedd came from the ground.

"It was... foolish. I wanted to deny you the three things that would make you a man. Your own name, weapons to carry and a wife," Arianrhod said. "For that I am sorry. I wanted to stop you from becoming like my brother and the King."

Lleu held his mother's hands and forgave her. Now, after all these years, he understood her plight completely. Arianrhod turned her head to Blodeuwedd.

"You are to marry my son?"

Blodeuwedd looked at Lleu, who felt as equally despondent about the situation as she did. She sighed and Lleu kept his head low. Arianrhod looked from Blodeuwedd to her son and realised quickly that they were not, as she assumed, madly in love with one another. This marriage looked like the last thing in the world that they wanted to do.

"It is what Gwydion wants," Blodeuwedd said.

"What is it that you want, Blodeuwedd?" Lleu asked her.

"To be free."

Arianrhod held her hand and they heard movement outside of Blodeuwedd's bedroom door and fear gripped them. The door opened and Arianrhod's suspicions were confirmed when Gwydion stepped foot through the door and into the room. He wore his finest tunic for the wedding and his blonde hair was combed back without a single strand out of place.

"Sister. What a surprise," Gwydion said. He slammed the door shut behind him and shot Lleu an angry glare.

"They don't want this marriage, Gwydion. You are foolish to force it on them," Arianrhod said.

"I think you are the last person to begin calling people fools," Gwydion said. "You should have taken your chance for freedom when I gave it to you. Instead, you have chosen to die."

When Gwydion began his spell, Lleu reached for his sword. Before he managed to take it out, Arianrhod grabbed the knife that was sheathed in the belt of her dress and lunged for Gwydion. She sank the knife into the centre of his chest, aiming for his heart, and stared into the green of his eyes.

Gwydion staggered and Arianrhod shoved the knife further into his chest. His mouth, agape, closed before he plummeted to the floor. Caught off his guard, Arianrhod watched his eyes widen slightly before slackening. Arianrhod pulled the knife from his heart and blood oozed from the wound. The side of his lip began to run red down to the crook of his neck. She moved away from the corpse and dropped the knife to the floor with a clatter.

Lleu stared at Gwydion's lifeless body, expecting the pang of grief to hit his chest. It never came. He watched the blood pooling around the wound near his heart and felt nothing. He raised his eyes to Arianrhod and felt relief for what she had done. Blodeuwedd couldn't speak nor move for shock. Her creator lay motionless on the floor and she suddenly felt free.

They left the King's court and found horses to escape. Finding Goewin hidden away, they stopped for breath. They knew that, soon, Gwydion's body would be found and that they would be the first suspects.

"Go now, my son, my Lleu," Arianrhod said.

"But what will the three of you do?" Lleu asked.

"If Blodeuwedd so wishes, she may join us and we will find our freedom," Arianrhod said. "Go now and live your life. Never forget the women who spared you."

"I will see you again."

"That is our final tynged. We will see each other again," Arianrhod said.

Lleu held onto his mother's hands and thanked her. When he left on horseback, the three women made their way in the opposite direction. They left behind the court, their homes and everything that they knew. The guards would find Gwydion's body in Blodeuwedd's room and run for the King. They would find that Lleu and Blodeuwedd had gone and the King would assume they left together for freedom from Gwydion's magical clutches. He would be short of a magician and so search the lands for another. They would never know the truth of what happened on that day.

When they left Gwynedd, their hearts soared with the prospect of a new beginning. The flowers in Blodeuwedd's hair fell out of her hair and wedding dress as they rode far, far away. They travelled off the beaten track and into lands where nobody would know them.

Blodeuwedd drank in the new sights like a newborn child and held onto Arianrhod's waist for dear life. Goewin led the way and they decided to keep travelling south. They had faced so many horrors as women and hoped to begin a new life with joy. Arianrhod couldn't think of any life better than living in harmony with the land and with each other.

In the distance, the sun began to rise over the brow of the hill. Blodeuwedd watched the flowers begin to fold open as the light of the sun began to touch their petals. Goewin and Arianrhod held each other's hands and watched Blodeuwedd, who was overjoyed by the sun's arrival. She rose with the flowers and watched the sun, once peeking over the hill, arrive fully in the sky. Goewin and Arianrhod rose to hold Blodeuwedd's hands and they thanked the sun for another day of freedom.

CASTING IN BLOOD

EL ROSE

El Rose is a writer of all things fantastical, queer, and complicated. Inspired by everything she sees and hears, El writes to explore character dynamics and relationships in her works whether they take form in novels, poems, or short stories. When not writing one of her simultaneously ongoing literary projects, El can be found enjoying DnD podcasts and teaching her cat to sit on her shoulders. Previously unpublished, El aims to spend a year out before starting her master's degree in order to finish her latest novel and see where it takes her.

For my Mum. I love you loads and loads too. Thank you.

LET ME TELL YOU A STORY OF TWO SISTERS AND A LOVER. A TALE of letters received too late and magic that wasn't enough. It is one you may be familiar with; it echoes on the cries of the winds around here. A ghost's regrets poured out to whoever can hear her when the veil between worlds is thin, when the shadows of the trees grow longer, stretching with grasping fingers towards the candlelight in your windows, craving warmth in the darkness. You may know of whispers from grandparents who lived in the time before you were a thought in a mind. Have you been to the ruins of that manor house? Crumbling stones that tremble in a storm, threatening to fall down to the dead grass in charred heaps. Did you pass off the cold spot in what once was the most welcoming entrance hall in Wales as a chill from lack of walls? A thought, an excuse, a desperate reasoning to stop the goosebumps from rising along your arms. Did you wave away the howling of grief that chilled your blood as nothing but a gust of wind through crumbled rocks and wooden beams? Did you turn away from learning her story? Did you leave her like the others?

I ask you to hear it now. To listen and to learn from her tragedy.

Years ago, a century or two or five it feels like now, there stood a manor house on the outskirts of a hearty valley village. Wreathed by garden plots left to run wild with heathers and dandelions, sweet-peas climbing up the fences, ladybirds and bees and apple trees with robin's nests. Rooms with warm hearths and soft rugs under bare feet. Windows that shone like a lighthouse during winter, calling those in need to rest at their stoop.

In this ruling home lived a widow, pregnant with a bump larger than she expected for one lonely child. Shuffling from her bed to her parlour and back, rarely going further than the bench in her front garden. Exhaustion setting in quick, and feet swollen until they burned, she was becoming a recluse. After her husband's death, the village had gone into mourning with her for having lost such a generous man but whilst she stayed swathed in black silks and a house too quiet for the space it commanded, those in the community below started emerging once more. Mourning more than grieving. Living life to the fullest as they always had.

"Twins," the village witch told her when she paid a visit, a soothing smile on her young face.

The mother could not help the twist of fear from showing on her face. The witch, with golden hair and knowing eyes, saw her terror and made a vow upon the magic in her veins, the scars that danced across her face and neck.

"Do not fret," she said, taking the mother's hands in hers, "I will get you through these births alive. I have done it before, you know I have, and I can do it again. I promise you; these children will not be orphaned as they are born. I will keep you breathing."

And so, she did.

She worked tirelessly when the night came. With the eldest and wisest of the village people around her, the young healer cast spell after charm after enchantment. Mixed potion after balm after salve. But a witch's power comes with a price, as all things in nature must remain balanced. With every casting a new fractal cut would carve itself into her skin, beads of blood blooming like blossoms and growing into an unstoppable river. Her husband, standing at her back and tucking her hair from her sweat-soaked brow, begged her to rest. To take a break. She refused. She had made a promise to the mother and refused to stop giving her aid even as a particularly taxing spell took the sight from her left eye. Even when her husband wept into the nape of her neck, trying to staunch a cut across her stomach. Even when the world spun around her. She kept working her casting until two little girls were born, safe and sound, and the mother was stitched together. Tired but well.

Only then did she let herself collapse, the room and rags and the clothing she wore stained more by her own blood than by that of the mother's. Her husband caught her with a cry of fear and relief.

The healer never woke again.

She was succeeded by her own young daughter, a girl named after her father's favourite flower: Yarrow, and her husband. For nearly a year, he could not speak his lost wife's name through his grief. Could do nothing but care for his daughter as if she too would pass before his very eyes if he were not careful.

In respect to the healer's sacrifice, the mother named the first of her daughters after the healer and so one of the sisters of our tale, Lilian, came to be in the shadow of grief. Her second daughter she named after her childhood friend, Marian.

For years, the manor house was full of laughter and light. Marian and Lilian lived in each other's pockets, as twins tend to do. Identical in every way, their mischief was known to all who cared for them. The same brown eyes, the same tilt to their shoulders, the same unusual height. Always together, always doting on their aging mother as they grew. The village people would see them often up above the side of the valley, climbing trees in ripped dresses and following their mother like fledgling chicks as she checked in on the lands under her reign. She ran the farmsteads fairly and there were few complaints even in the last of the tavern's drinking hours when all workers love to come together to lament the fate of working life. She and her children were loved by all.

All except for the healer's husband.

He kept his daughter away from the girls, the only others of her age in the village, for many reasons. Grief is not so easy a thing to understand, it makes people act on logic that is born of a broken heart. The motivation grief provides isn't simple to explain to others, no matter how much a storyteller may wish it were. And so, with few friends and fewer peers to play with, Yarrow grew quickly into a mature, hard-working girl. Learning what her father could remember of his wife's skills with poultices and trying to teach herself to cast spells found in books around the house. She would see the twins from afar, dream wistfully of having a sister of her own. A friend of her own. The boys of the village fawned over Yarrow. Asking her to the dances held at the manor but she always answered the same.

'My father does not like me being away long.'

It was true, after all, if not the total truth. She was far more interested with her books, her spells, her potions. The twins, though, would twirl and bat their eyes at the boys. Playfight in the fields with them. Go on adventures with sticks for swords with them into the woods.

But it was not Yarrow's fate to be the next witch of the valley. That burden fell upon Marian when she turned of age at the innocence of her thirteenth year.

Marian watched, thirteen and unknowing of magic beyond tales of the healer who saved her mother, as her sister ran away, broken-but-somehow-now-fixed wooden doll clasped to her chest, crying for their mother. Blood dripped from a mysterious cut above Marian's left eyebrow. She swiped at it as it dripped onto her lashes, frustrated in her lack of understanding, staring at the smear of red on the backs of her knuckles. She had seen blood before, had had plenty of grazes and falls and accidents. But this… It hurt. It hurt a lot. But she was much more concerned with what had coursed through her just a moment before. She had wanted to fix the damage she'd done to her sister's doll in a fit of childish rage and suddenly, like the sun had shone and she could see everything sharp and clear as a summer day, her hands, her fingers, had known the dance. Had worked and tugged on something she'd never felt but was somehow all around her in the air now. She'd fixed the doll. And now she bled.

Marian walked, hand clasped in sweaty hand with Lilian, following their mother leading them to a house they had never been to before in the village. Their mother hesitated, taking a deep breath, before knocking resolutely. Lilian shifted, tugging closer to Marian as they waited for whoever could be inside, little fingers curling tight around her forearm. Marian was expecting an old woman, wrinkled and dusty, creaking as she moved. Lilian pictured a man, middle-aged like how she imagined a father must be, a greying short beard and warm smile. Their mother did not seem surprised when a girl their age opened the door, a sure if a little confused smile on her lips. A bread knife in one hand, seemingly forgotten in her haste to greet her guests, crumbs still sticking to it and on the apron tied around her waist.

Marian would declare, quiet and sure, at her hand-fasting in a few years' time that it was at this moment that she fell in love. Yarrow would tell her in return that she knew Marian was it for her when Marian had embroidered a ribbon for her hair from a strip of cloth from her own shirt just because Yarrow had loved the colour.

At the time, Yarrow called for her father who appeared behind her. Looming large and fitting Lilian's expectations in every way. A father. She felt a pang of jealousy as he dropped a hand on his daughter's shoulder. She turned to see if her sister felt the same conflict in her own heart but found nothing but simple awe on her sister's face. Her full attention on this other girl. Her hand slipping from Lilian's own as if she didn't remember she even had a twin anymore. This, Lilian would later know, was when she had lost her sister.

Yarrow's father, seeing it was pointless and not wishing to defile his wife's memory, agreed reluctantly to let Marian read through Yarrow's inherited books. To let his daughter, his last remaining family, and the strongest reminder of his beloved wife, enter the lives of the woman who had been the cause of his wife's demise. She would not have wanted him to wallow in anger and hatred. It had been her choice. Now, he knew, he must let his daughter make her own choices too.

And so, Marian learnt to cast, and Lilian watched from the sidelines as her other half became absorbed in spellwork. At her mother's behest, she heeded almost every warning Yarrow's mother had left behind. Yarrow, herself, became a part of the family like she had never been kept away. When Marian wanted to play, it was to Yarrow, no longer Lilian, that she turned. When she woke from night terrors, it was Yarrow she looked for instead of the twin sister sharing her bed. When Marian had a secret to share, Yarrow was the one who knew it. Yarrow with her darling dimples. Yarrow with her smart glasses handed down from Marian and Lilian's own father. Each change, each announcement of Yarrow's presence, each excited rambling from Marian about her dear friend Yarrow, tore at Lilian like it was a magic all its own.

Day by day, week by week, Lilian was forgotten by Marian as any more than a clingy sister. A sister desperate for attention from anyone who would give it. Whilst Lilian watched their mother become ill, powerless to do anything at age sixteen and only having learnt to tame the foals and fashion molten metal safely, Marian- Marian was off rolling around in the hay with her childhood sweetheart.

Lilian mopped their mother's fever-stricken brow. Marian bled to create shows of tiny lights to make Yarrow laugh.

Lilian was there to be a shoulder to cry on for their mother's hysterics. Marian was busy having tea at Yarrow's house.

Lilian cried herself to sleep at their mother's bedside. Marian came home drunk when the sun was beginning to rise again, bruises from Yarrow's mouth on her neck shown off like medals.

Lilian was there. Marian was not.

Lilian was alone, as their mother's hand turned cold. Marian was sleeping in Yarrow's bed.

~

After their mother's funeral, Lilian no longer tried to hide her resentment towards her sister. For all the gifts and power she had been given, Marian rarely used it for anything useful. Lilian cursed the weavings of fate for not giving her the crafts of a witch. She would have helped the crops grow when they failed before winter. She would have fashioned gold for the village people to travel and trade with. She would have saved their mother.

Still, for all her fury, Marian did not notice Lilian's hostility.

Lilian was left with no choice at all when Marian announced her intentions to marry Yarrow. Lilian left the day of the wedding. Slipping away with her pack and her wits. A part of her heart died that night as she left her sister and all remaining love for her behind.

~

These torn sisters of our tale did not see each other again for ten years.

Marian awoke, the day after her wedding, to a note on their dining room table and a room empty of any personal belongings. Memories hounded her for months, flickers of Lilian in the corners of rooms, shouting to share a joke with her across the dancefloor at a ball held in their home, nightmares of her sister dying, scared and alone in some marsh or plague-ridden town. Eventually, Yarrow had had enough. What should have been one of the happiest times of their lives, newlywed and living together at last, was overshadowed by the loss of Lilian. Sometimes, when drunk and roaming the house as if expecting Lilian to be in every other room, Marian would shout theories, what-ifs about where she'd gone. What if she'd been taken? What if she'd eloped with a paramour? What if - What if - What if - One morning, the scorching summer sun having woken Yarrow earlier than her wife, Marian walked downstairs to find her traveling bag packed and her horse saddled, ready for a long journey. Yarrow waved her off with a kiss and a heartfelt wish of luck.

So, she started to search for her sister every spring, leaving her wife behind to take off out of the valley, looking far and wide to fix the mistakes she finally could take responsibility for. She wanted nothing more than to explain the fear she had lived with when they had been young. How the story of Yarrow's mother's death and the horrors of other witches' lives had left her frozen. Terrified to do more than the small spells Yarrow coaxed her to try. How she had avoided their sick mother because of the guilt that kept her up all night for her own failing at being a witch. Her own miserable destiny. She wanted to apologise. She needed to try to make things right. If only Lilian would let her.

When they did reunite, towards the end of spring in the tenth year of her search, just as Marian was giving up hope for the season, it was not pretty.

There was not the warm embrace for which she had hoped. There was not the long, difficult but ultimately worth it conversation of which she had dreamed. There was not a relieved smile on her sister's face and there was not a feeling of coming home in her chest.

Instead, Marian stumbled, weary and blinking her eyes until they started to water just to keep them open, into what she had supposed to be an empty hay barn. Over the years she had gained muscle from her excursions, become accustomed to less-than-ideal sleeping arrangements, learnt the local dialects of the surrounding towns and villages outside of her home valley. She was on the outskirts of the furthest seaport she had ever reached, heart heavy and horse hungry. A local farmhand had directed her here, to a barn that was well known in the village to be rarely used by its owners.

'No one will mind,' they had said, 'it stores hay and seed and barely even that.'

It was not empty. She wished it had been. Down to her bones, she wished she were more surprised by what she found. Marian didn't hesitate in what she did next. Not when the scene before her could not be interpreted in any other way. Her arm bled profusely, a show of such proportion taking a heavy cost. One that would require a proper salve and wrapping. It bled through her shirt and dripped down her wrist, down her fingers, pooling on the floor. Drip. Staining the strands of hay. Drip. Warm. Sticky in the heat. Drip.

The milkmaid ran past her, cheeks flushed and sobs hitching in her chest. Pink spring festival dress torn. Ruined. She grasped Marian's hand as she passed, flinching away with a shocked gasp as she felt the blood, saw it on her own bruised skin. She left without looking back.

Marian couldn't stop staring at the body on the hay. So still. Silent. No injuries or signs of illness to mark a natural death. Because it hadn't been. She had done this. Her hands had formed the steps without a second thought. She was a murderer. Yarrow could never touch her again; she could not taint her with what she'd done. She could never again hold Yarrow close after a night terror about her mother. Never kiss her brow as they parted for the day. Never dance for hours on end under sparkling lights. Never.

Lilian would understand. Lilian would know. The boys in the village when they were young had not been kind, not in the end. Marian and Lilian had learnt this the hard way. Three of her scars were from protecting herself and her sister from unwanted hands and cruel threats. It had never ended in death, until now. Three. Now four. Find Lilian. She had to find Lilian. Lilian would wash the blood from her soul, just as she had each time before. Lilian would build her back together. She could not go home until she had.

Drip.

There was no way to tell how long she'd been there before the last of her hopes crumbled around her.

A voice in the field outside. Hundreds of memories of fireside whispers. The thudding of running feet. Scars from games played with childhood imagination. A name, a man's name called again and again. Fingers itching to hold her sister, soothe her dangerous tone, solve the hurt. The thump of a body hitting into the door, pushing it further open in a rush. A stillness. The scrape of shoes sliding to an unexpected stop. The rush of air and the clenching of familiar fists.

"You."

Marian's voice did not shake. "Me."

"What have you done?" Lilian demanded; she couldn't see the body past Marian, not yet. "Milly came into the house screaming her head off about some witch in the barn and what she'd done to my-" The shuffle of hay and the clack of a heel. "To my... " Another step.

Marian balled her hands into fists, relishing the tear of the cut skin further up her arm.

"My husband."

"He was forcing himself on her. I couldn't let-"

Lilian pushed past her, shoulder ramming into her own so hard that Marian tipped, hitting a post but managing to stay upright. The cut screamed, agony flaring. Lilian collapsed next to her husband's body, tears of rage in her eyes as she stroked his hair. Marian swallowed back her nausea.

"She was asking for it," Lilian said, nearly whispered, Marian couldn't bear to see her sister weep over the man, but she knew to intervene would be to wreck their reunion even more. "Always flirting with him. Batting her damned eyelashes up at him when she brought the milk in. He was just- He's - He was a man! She was-"

"No!" Marian cried, cutting in at last. "No, she wasn't! She cried for help, Lilian, how do you not see that?"

"Stop it."

"You know I'm - she's telling the truth. We've been her, Lilian, how can you say that?"

"Get out."

Marian didn't move. Couldn't move. This wasn't how it was supposed to go. Lilian wasn't supposed to be married to some- some farm boy rapist. Lilian wasn't supposed to look up at her over a corpse, meeting her gaze for the first time with ice in her gaze. Her eyes, their eyes, were cold and dark as a frozen lake.

"Get. Out." Lilian repeated, practically growling at her. "Now!"

Marian did.

She could not go home. Not with knowing the life she had taken, for good reason or not. Not without Lilian now she was so close, close enough to touch. She could never touch Yarrow again, could not bear to see Yarrow forgive her so easily like Marian knew she would. So, she fled to the nearest town where she knew no one and no one knew her. She wrote one letter to be sent home. To tell Yarrow all that had happened, that she would be home when she could. If she could.

~

Lilian did not bury her husband. She had no love lost for him, not truly. Marian had more than likely been right about his crimes, but Lilian was sick, sick to the marrow in her bones of her sister causing misery without experiencing any herself. Of coming in and taking things from her without a care. It was easy to give herself over entirely to the rage, building since that fateful day when a girl and her father opened the door. No magic would save Marian from her sister's wrath.

~

Knowing Marian so well, it was with ease that she tracked her sister down. She had not gotten far, giving in to her exhaustion a couple of fields away along the road back to the seaport. With a steady heart and silent step, Lilian stood over her sister's sleeping body. Silver scars glowing oddly in the moonlight. Shadows casting her face into something strange, inhuman. Witch, she thought, a witch. She'd known what her sister was. Of course, she'd known. But to see her now. Blood stains on her clothes, cloth gauze wrapped around one arm. Hands under her head. This was not the sister she played hide and seek with. This was not the sister she loved with the fire of the sun. This was not her sister. This was a witch and nothing more. It was easy too, to take her sister's pack and horse, leaving no sign of herself behind.

And it was with a steady heart and no remorse that Lilian burnt Marian's letter to Yarrow and cut her hair to match the witch's. It was as easy as breathing to mimic her walk, talk as she talked, smile as she did. The only issue in her assumed identity was her lack of scars. Where Marian was riddled with them like an intricate lace hem, Lilian had not a one. She didn't have to fool everyone. Just one person. The person who thought she knew Marian better than Lilian did. It was possible.

With a horse and a head start, Lilian returned to her birthplace in good time. No doubt the witch would follow after her, but it would take her longer. She would not push her horse to ride through the night until its mouth was flecked with foam, eyes rolling wide in its skull. Lilian would. Lilian had. The manor stood quiet in the dawn's meager light. No candles burned in the windows. The curtains pulled. The doors locked. She stabled the horse on her own, unwilling to take the risk of waking the staff Yarrow and the witch kept and being discovered before she could complete the last of her preparations.

Marian's pack had her own house key in it and Lilian used it to slip quietly into the house. She made her way upstairs, fingers gliding over the wooden banister, nails dragging across the walls. The doorknob was cold under her palm. It groaned as she pushed, but nothing stirred. The curtains kept the room in a soft darkness. She curled her toes in the rug at the foot of the bed. Tilted her head as she observed the sleeping figure, curled slightly, facing towards the empty side next to her. Silk sheets outlining her slight body. Hair wild across the pillows. One freckled shoulder poking out, bare, from the covers. A bird called outside.

Lilian took the pair of glasses from the nightstand. Broke the bridge in half, slipped them into her pockets. To dispose of them somewhere would risk someone finding them, revealing that things weren't right. Yarrow's vision had been fading fast since they were still young, without the glasses all she would see was her wife. The scars would be an issue if Yarrow tried to touch her but all that required was long sleeves and keeping her face from being touched. Easy. It was all too easy. The witch would return in a couple of days. All she had to do was keep up the facade until then.

~

Yarrow woke to another body beside her in bed. Their back turned to her, travel-short hair dusting the pillow, winter night-gown on. It must have been cold last night, Yarrow thought, when she returned, at least she is home now. She shuffled closer, wrapping herself around her wife's body, pressing kisses between her shoulder blades. Another year of no success. It wasn't unexpected. But it wasn't welcome. Marian stirred in her arms, arching back into her with the familiarity of years of life together.

"You're home," Yarrow mumbles against the cloth covering her wife's back. "What time did you get in?"

"Early this morning."

"You could have woken me."

Marian hummed, turning to face Yarrow who couldn't see much more than the outlines of her face, the colours that made her up, without her glasses.

"I missed you."

"I missed you too, my love," Yarrow whispered, stealing a morning kiss.

The morning passed as any other first morning home after Marian's search. Warm, languid touches. Reassurances of love and care. Compassion for the failure of her quest once again. Yarrow, after, left Marian to sleep and recover. Told the servants to leave her be for a couple of days, as was the routine. Knowing that Marian would be asleep for at least the rest of the day, Yarrow walked down to her father's house to pay a visit and announce her wife's return. He was always anxious when she was left to live in the old manor on her own. Too much loneliness, he said. That morning, he welcomed her with a kind hug and a promise of a cooked breakfast. She kept the fact that she'd already eaten to herself.

"Marian is home," she said, accepting a cup of tea from him with a kiss to his cheek.

"Ah, that is good news. When did she get back?"

"This morning, I was still asleep."

"This morning. Isn't that a bit soon?"

Yarrow frowned, taking a sip of her drink before replying, "is it?"

"I had thought she would be another week at least," he said, something in his tone setting Yarrow on edge, "did something happen?"

"No?"

He shot her a disbelieving look over his shoulder. "You don't sound so sure on that."

"She's fine," Yarrow insisted. "Just as normal."

"Fine," he relented, holding a hand up in surrender, "where are your glasses, anyway?"

"Misplaced them, I think. They weren't where I thought I'd put them. But I'm managing well enough!" Her father closed his mouth, looking slightly chastened. "Don't worry about me. It's for me to worry about you, old man."

When she returned home later in the afternoon, her father's words were still whispering in the back of her mind. It was early, really. She had also anticipated Marian being away for another couple of weeks, and to return but not wake her was unusual too. But surely it was just the stress of travel? Of her sister's loss being so fresh around this time of year? To distract herself from such ridiculous concerns she joined up with the housekeeper to search for her glasses but to no avail. They were gone. Perhaps dropped from a pocket when she was walking round the gardens the night before, a headache had forced her to take them off and she couldn't remember putting them back on.

Marian emerged around dinner time. Dressed in an old dress and housecoat. She asked about her glasses, but Marian hadn't seen them either. It wasn't until it was truly dark outside, and they were curled up together on the lounge in front of the drawing room fire that the feeling that something was wrong crept back in like a whisper in Yarrow's mind. Marian had said little all evening, playing with Yarrow's hair and pressing the occasional kiss to the line of her jaw. She knew that she'd left a bruise on Marian's neck this morning but for once she had covered it up. Odd in and of itself but it shouldn't be enough to have her stomach twisting in knots.

When there was a loud, aggressive knock at the door, Yarrow startled to her feet. Marian didn't even flinch. If she was able to see better, Yarrow would have sworn there was a smile on her face.

"Who is it? Are we expecting someone?" Yarrow asked, confused and more than a little scared as whoever it slammed against the door again.

"No, my dear, but we shall certainly go see who it is. They must have some pressing matter to discuss if they're here this late."

Marian rose and took Yarrow's hand in hers. Her gloved hand. Why was she wearing gloves indoors? In their own home? Why hadn't Yarrow noticed before? She was about to ask when Marian pulled her into the hallway, not so gently. Yarrow followed, trying not to trip over her own dress skirts and feet. The knocking was constant, with the occasional crack as if someone were kicking the door as well. Yarrow shied back into Marian's chest. Marian held her close, arms around her front, holding her tight. There was something cold in Marian's sleeve, hard where it pressed into Yarrow's stomach. She covered Marian's gloved hands with her own.

"They'll let themselves in soon, I'm sure."

"What?" Yarrow asked, trying to twist to look at her wife's face, to try to understand what was going on but Marian would not let her. "Why don't we just call out and ask?"

"We can wait."

"Marian, I don't understand."

"I know."

"Marian! You're starting to hurt me, let go."

Marian just hummed. The fear in Yarrow's blood was crystalising into terror.

"Marian! What-"

The door split down the middle with an unearthly sound.

A figure, lit by the light of the hallway. Blood blooming down their face, from temple to the curve of her neck.

"Marian?" Yarrow breathed.

Pain. A sharp pain. Then another. Again. And again.

A gasp. A scream. Rage and pain and grief and horror and shock and hers. Marian's. And a laugh. At last, a laugh. Lilian's laugh.

~

Marian watched, rooted in place, as Lilian stabbed the knife into Yarrow's stomach over and over and over again. Blood spilling onto the floor and why could she hear it? Were you meant to hear it? And taste it in the air? And smell the sickly metal stench already? Lilian was laughing. She was laughing and not stopping.

Then she wasn't.

The last thing Lilian saw was her sister. Her twin. Herself reflected back at her across a room. At last, the pain that Lilian had lived with for so long reflected on the witch's face.

Marian snapped out of her frozen state as Lilian's body hit the floor, dragging Yarrow down with her. She was across the room in an instant, pulling Yarrow's arm, her waist, her shoulders, trying to get her away from Lilian as quickly as possible. Her knees jarred painfully as she hit the ground alongside Yarrow, unable to move her far enough away or pull her to stand.

"Yarrow, come on, help me out here," she begged, tears blurring her vision and there was a tinge of red too? She swiped it away but more fell in its place until she was pretty sure she was looking through only her right eye. It didn't matter. "Yarrow, come on, come on, darling."

No response. She tugged Yarrow into her lap, cradled her cheek, patting lightly.

"Wake up, look at me. Look at me, come on, please, Yarrow, please, my love…"

She dipped her head to Yarrow's mouth, listening for a sound.

Any sound. A breath. A whisper of a word. Anything.

Nothing.

She moved to try to find a heartbeat, her ear over her lover's breast, a litany of apologies falling from her lips without her notice. Apologies for bleeding on her dress. Apologies for not catching her. Apologies for not just letting Lilian go.

Nothing.

Heat was starting to flicker up her back, as if she were facing away from the hearth. She didn't move to look.

She didn't move even as the heat moved up her neck, set her brain on fire. Sparked down to her fingers, clenched still around Yarrow. Yarrow who wasn't sitting up. Yarrow who wasn't answering her. Yarrow who wasn't breathing- oh god- she wasn't- she's not-

Someone was screaming. Hoarse and wild and loud, echoing through the hall, echoing out the broken door of the broken home. The heat was becoming unbearable. Marian refused to move. The thought did not even occur to her. She was too wrapped up in Yarrow to care for the pain in her throat, her knees, the cuts shredding her skin like she was being unraveled.

The three of them burned together. Two bodies were found the next morning by the village people, but it was clear that only magic, raw, pain-fueled magic could have sparked and fed such a raging blaze. The house had burned down with them.

And so, that is the story of the manor ruins up the gravel path. That is who you can hear howling in the night, following you in the dark. Two sisters and a lover. A witch, a wife, and a widow, haunting a valley with their tragedy.

THAT WHICH FOLLOWS
YOU BACK
MATTHIAS BOLATA

Matthias Bolata is a writer from Belgium who is
currently residing in North Wales, completing their
postgraduate degree in Creative Writing at Bangor University. He is interested in exploring the
boundaries between the real and the fantastical in
their own writing.

To my fellow writers who helped encourage me.

"Did you hear? Did you hear?"
"Did you hear the rumour about the thing on Owens Road that follows your back?"

T HEY SAY THAT IF YOU GO DOWN OWENS ROAD ALONE AT NIGHT, you might just hear the sound of someone walking behind you.

Owens Road is a quiet, suburban road that leads into the city, around a mile and a half in length. Houses dominate both sides of the road – away from the hustle and bustle of the city, yet close enough for it to be a convenient walking distance. Quite a few people go along this road for various reasons, although hardly ever did someone actually go down it at night. Yet those who do, of course, occasionally have a story to tell to those who might want to listen.

At first, it might be barely noticeable. Yet, as you continue walking down the long residential street, you might catch it. With each and every step you take, you might hear someone just behind you take a step at the exact moment as you did. Each time your foot lands on the sidewalk, whoever or whatever is behind you takes another step as well, precisely coordinated with your own. It is almost as if it is mirroring your own footsteps.

The further along the road you go, the sound of the steps may seem to come closer and seem to get louder, until it is almost as if it is walking right behind you.

If this happens, you should just continue walking — not run, never running — and never stop until you reach home and close the door.

And whatever you do, you shouldn't look back to see what is following you. Not until you are in the safety of your own home, which it cannot seem to reach.

Of course, that's just a rumour. Less than a rumour, even. Rumours may have some basis in reality that set them apart from fiction — something that makes it plausible enough to seem like it actually happened. Therefore, such a story, with its implausibility, would not be able to match up to being a rumour.

This is no more than a fable, then. It isn't something you should put any stock in once you've become an adult. Stories like these come and go all the time, yet there is never any proof that anything like them ever actually happened, any evidence that what is being said is actually the case. Fables, urban legends, folklore, and so on. They are all the same. They are nothing more than stories meant to scare children and keep them in line, make sure they don't leave their houses.

Stories like these go back generations, and they shift and adapt according to what parents want to dissuade their children from doing. 'Don't go near the river, or otherwise the old lady who lives in the river will drag you in', for example, is a story meant to stop children from accidentally drowning. Similarly, stories are built up in order to dissuade children from staying out late, and to get home as soon as possible after it becomes dark. These are universal.

As children, when we are told by our parents that something isn't safe because a monster lives there, we naturally will believe them. As we grow up, we will discard these stories as made-up fictions, yet acknowledge the value that they might once have had. We understand that there isn't really an old lady in the river, yet we can still acknowledge the real danger that our parents might have been trying to warn us about. The river will still drag us away, not because of an old lady, but rather because of the flow.

Fables like these are a shield meant to protect children from harm, to push them along and keep them on the right path, and to ensure that they continue to come home safe and sound.

~

"Do you really think all that?" Rhys asks me. We are walking down Owens Road, as we usually do, and the subject of the urban legend attached to the location came up for one reason or another.

"Of course, I do. If one thinks about it rationally, it was the only way it made sense." I explain to him, hoping it would let him see things from my point of view. Rhys furrows his brows and turns to look in front of him, but he doesn't say anything at first. Briefly, I think I must have convinced him with my explanations, which was rather relieving, as it meant there didn't need to be a further discussion, and we could move on.

Then he brings something up I didn't quite expect to hear.

"Shaun says he's seen it – well, not seen seen it, but you know what I mean."

"Has he now?" I wonder out loud. That was rather surprising. Shaun has always seemed like a rather reasonable fellow; I have always thought this. He always keeps his head on his shoulders, and never acts irrationally beyond a few of his habits. He didn't ever strike me as someone so childish as to believe in stories like this – much less claim that he experienced one for himself.

"Yeah, he told me about it once when we were having a drink at the Laurels. You weren't there, though." Rhys' shrugs his shoulders awkwardly, putting his hands in his pockets. I don't go drinking with the two of them, as I am strictly sober, and don't particularly like the environment of pubs, so I nod at what he says without further comment. This did make sense as to why I hadn't heard of it before now.

"Anyways, Shaun says he's seen it, and I believe him." Sticking with this, Rhys seems to be digging in his heels, which was rather frustrating.

Why should I believe Shaun, I almost say back, but I hold my tongue. Shaun is our senior at our job, and older than the both of us, and so I held a great deal of respect for him. So, even if I don't believe he'd seen it – well, I couldn't outright say it like that. I believe him over a great deal other things, after all. So, I can't say 'why should I believe him'. I think over it, rephrasing what I was about to say.

"If he didn't see it, how can he say that he saw anything at all?" I instead ask, deciding that was much more of a diplomatic way of phrasing it than my first thought.

Rhys looks back at me, frowning again while trying to figure out what I meant by that. For a while, I am afraid what I had said might have upset him, which wasn't my intention, as it seemed to take a while. When he finally spoke up again, though, there doesn't seem to be anything different about the way he is speaking – he had just been thinking it over, which I am thankful for.

"Well, he could hear it, probably. That's one of the things in all the stories, right? How you can hear it following your footsteps and all that? So that's probably it."

I still am not convinced, however. Shaking my head, I feel a smile creeping along my lips; I hadn't intended to. I can't really help myself, when I am explaining things like this — the rush that I get from proving my point of view is far too enjoyable to not smile, after all.

"He probably was mishearing things."

Rhys looks back over at me again, the doubt evident on his face. He must be thinking that I was being a bit of a twat, but that didn't bother me all that much. It wasn't as if I was dismissing everything that Shaun had experienced, which meant I wasn't calling him a liar. So long as I was framing it as if he wasn't lying intentionally, but rather subconsciously misunderstanding what he experienced, the conversation wouldn't get any more heated.

"What makes you say that?"

"The human mind is easier to trick than most people realize," I begin, and Rhys looks at me intently, as if to judge my answer, "It's easy for us to think we heard something, but in reality it was nothing at all. For example — have you ever heard anybody ever call your name out of nowhere, even when there is no obvious source?"

Rhys seems to stop and think for a moment, as if trying to recall if he had had any such moments in his life. Before too long, he nods his head slowly.

At that, I let myself smile just a little more, and I continue with my explanation.

"Like I said, the human mind is easier to trick than people realize. So, you heard someone calling your name, even though there was no obvious source. This is because you heard a noise — maybe someone saying or shouting something from a distance, for example — which your mind then registered and processed. However, because you didn't hear it properly, you subconsciously attempt to seek familiar words that might sound similar to what was actually heard or spoken."

And what is most familiar to us if not our own names?

"I guess that makes sense, if you put it like that. But how does that explain what Shaun heard?"

"Well, I can only guess at that — but I think he was probably hearing the sound of his own footsteps."

"He was hearing his own footsteps?" Rhys raises an eyebrow, the doubt evident in his tone of voice. "Now that doesn't make any sense."

I shake my head and smile again despite myself. "It's similar to the explanation I gave before, I think. Rather than the mind subconsciously rearranging an unfamiliar sound into something familiar, it is rather that we process a familiar sound as unfamiliar."

Rhys again seems to take a moment to think over what I was saying in his head. I continue without hesitation, feeling rather satisfied with what I am saying, sure that I am getting my point across to him.

"Rather than hearing another pair of footsteps, I think it is possible Shaun was hearing his own footsteps, but he simply wasn't realizing it. Although, I can't say why he was walking as loudly as he was — but it's still a rational explanation for what might have happened. It's also a great deal more reasonable than some sort of ghost or bogeyman, I think."

It looks like Rhys is about to say something back at me, but he held it back for whatever reason. Pursing his lips for just a moment, he seems to be considering what I had said — or maybe he is thinking over what he is going to say in response. I can't quite tell either way.

"Well, let's see what Shaun thinks about it. I'm sure he'll have something to say about all of this."

It wasn't exactly what I had hoped to hear, but it is good enough for me for now. It wasn't as if I needed to convince Rhys right at this very moment. Rather, if I am to convince Shaun, I am sure Rhys would follow along with the two of our opinions. I have him pegged as that sort of person, and I hadn't seen anything yet to the contrary. Not to say he is easily swayed or anything — that'd be rude — but it was more like he is someone who would say yes in order to make things less complicated.

I appreciate that about him, in a way — that he holds himself back in order to accommodate for others. It makes him easier to talk to, and I think that is the reason I get along so well with him. It isn't a good thing, though, but it isn't quite a bad thing, either.

"I suppose I'll have to ask him, then." I'm finding it hard not to smile too widely, I realize as we continue walking. It wasn't that I am feeling particularly joyful right now, but the feeling that there was something to celebrate was undeniable. It is almost like the childlike urge to hop when something great happens to you.

The feeling of proving myself right is exhilarating, as it always is. It's an affirmation that my own views are sound and logical, through convincing others of their rationality. In this way, my discussion with Rhys was another affirmation that logic dictated the world rather than the fantastical.

The two of us make an unspoken agreement to drop the subject for now, and we continue on our way down Owens Road to work.

When we are about to take the corner off of Owens Road, I look back to where I had just been walking, confident in myself and what I believed in.

~

The opportunity to talk to Shaun about it didn't come up until our lunch break.

It is just the three of us who worked at our office, as it is just a small reception job that doesn't require many people, yet still pays decently enough for what it is. As a result, we end up eating lunch together more often than not, as we are the only people working there.

While he is chatting away with Rhys and mostly ignoring me for the moment, I am trying to think of how to best bring it up. I am hoping to not be too confrontational or accusatory towards him, while still wanting to make sure that there was some sort of conversation about this — I feel the need to bring it up, no matter how forceful it might be to do so.

The best way, as it turns out, is simply to bring it up at a point when the conversation seems to be dying down, and hope for the best.

"So, Rhys told me about that thing you encountered on Owens Road."

Shaun practically freezes in place, the sandwich he is just about to take a bite out of hanging in front of his mouth as his gaze shoots towards me, and then to Rhys, and then back to me. I can't really tell what he is thinking, but he seems annoyed. Maybe I had gone about it the wrong way, after all — but I couldn't exactly go back now that I had said it, so I had to push on.

"Did he now?" Shaun lowers his sandwich for a moment, before seeming to change his mind and taking a bite out of it anyways, looking directly at me while doing so.

"Well, we were talking about it, so it seemed like something to bring up at the time." Rhys excuses himself, glancing over at Shaun apologetically.

There is a brief silence between the three of us, as if neither of the other two wanted to continue speaking — but that isn't enough for me. I need to prove my own point of view to Shaun, in order to show him the truth of what he might have encountered. So, I push further.

"Are you really sure that it was, well, that, though?" I ask him, not sure how else to refer to it while still phrasing it delicately. I didn't want to seem too condescending, after all, or else Shaun might think I'm being disrespectful to him even though he is my senior.

Something about what I said seems to have annoyed Shaun regardless, though, despite my trying to be delicate. He looks over at me again, his large eyebrows burrowing themselves into his face and his eyes stares intently at me. It is slightly unnerving, to see him looking at me with such intensity, making me feel smaller than I actually am. Although, I suppose from his position, I am much smaller. I want to say something to ease the tension, but Shaun starts speaking before I can say anything at all.

"I know what happened that night, and I know for sure that whatever it was — it wasn't natural. So, yes, as far as I'm concerned. It was that."

"So, you didn't see it."

A silence falls over the three of us as both Shaun and Rhys look at me. It is almost as if there isn't any sound at all — but I knew that isn't possible. It is more as if I am unable to register the presence of any sound, as if my mind is focused entirely on this conversation between us three.

As far as I am concerned, the matter of whether or not his claim is credible hinged solely on if he had seen that thing on Owens Road with his own two eyes. If he had seen it, it would provide some form of evidence that his encounter had been more than just his mind playing tricks on him.

Therefore, the nature of this rumour is one where it remains undeniably true to the person in question so long as they do not look behind them. At the same time, it loses this quality if the person was to look behind them, as then they would be able to confirm or deny its existence.

Perhaps it would be incorrect to call it 'undeniably true' in the strict sense, then. Rather, it is more as if it is in between being true or false. In this sense, it is much like Schrödinger's Cat, where so long as a person did not look behind them, the possibilities of what is actually there would remain endless. Yet, once you looked back, it would confirm a single, definitive outcome, which would be 'undeniably true'.

This is why the urban legend has a built-in safety net, in order to allow it to continue its ambiguous nature. As stated in the rumour, it is important that the person never turns to look back if they feel like they are being followed by it. Otherwise, it will do 'something' to its intended victim. What exactly this 'something' is changes between retellings, but the most common one is invariably that it ends up killing the person. This is a rather easy incentive for a person to not turn back and to continue walking — after all, what reasonable person would want to turn around when to do so would be essentially risking their own life?

Of course, this also means that any such encounters with the thing where a person does turn around are also deniable. If a person who turned around claims that they did not see anything there, then although it was simply their imagination on that one occasion, that doesn't mean that that is the case every time. Something like that would surely be the line of argument that proponents of this rumour would go about trying to prove that this story was, in fact, true.

Naturally, the reason why there are no 'real' encounters from a person who turned around is simple: they simply befell the unfortunate yet vaguely defined fate that all its actual victims do.

As such, I feel that it is important to ask Shaun whether or not he had actually seen it. Although I already know the likely answer to this question, it is more important in my mind to put down the groundwork for future points that I might make, depending on how this conversation ends up going.

"No, of course I didn't see it. Why would I go and do that?" Shaun finally breaks the silence, and I feel a small bit of pride jump up in my chest as I lean just a little bit closer. I know exactly how to proceed from here, ready to go on the offensive and prove myself right. Even though it isn't as if this is an argument, it still is something I had confidence in that I could win.

That is, until he continues to talk.

"I didn't need to see it to know it was there, though. I could feel it."

I try to laugh it off as best as I could, despite my growing concern that this was not heading in the direction I had been anticipating. All the while, I keep glancing over at Rhys, who looks just as surprised as I felt about hearing this. Maybe Shaun hadn't told him — but why would he do something like that?

"What do you mean by that, exactly?" I tried to hide my nervousness by smiling when I ask him this, hoping that he doesn't notice. When he looks back at me and smiled back, I feel a rush of annoyance come over me, but I still try my best to stay civil and professional. After all, there isn't any use getting mad about something like this. It isn't real, anyway, I remind myself, so there is no harm in him spinning his little stories about what or what-did-not happen.

At the end of the day, I knew what the truth is, and he can't do anything to stop that — no matter what he might try and say to convince me.

"It wasn't as if it was touching me, don't get me wrong. But I could absolutely feel it. It was almost as if it was standing right behind me."

Before I can ask him for further clarification, Rhys, who had mostly been listening in up to this point, speaks up. "Why didn't you say this before, though?"

"Well, it wasn't as if I wasn't going to tell you. Just didn't really want to right then." Shaun shrugs and takes another bite of his sandwich, acting casually all the while. It is just a bit infuriating how little a deal he seems to be making about all of this.

"So, what happened?" Trying to get back on topic, I lean forward, eager to know what Shaun thought might have happened. It isn't as if he is going to convince me that it was actually the truth of the matter. Rather, I am interested in understanding what he perceived to be the truth.

His perception of events was necessary in order to establish the truth behind the urban legend. If it can be explained through rational means, I might be able to convince Shaun to see things from my point of view, as I had done with Rhys. It isn't as if it is my moral duty to do so, by any means, but I still thought of it as something important to do.

"I don't really want to talk about it." Shaun shuts me off, leaning back in his chair. I am about to say something to push ahead, but he glares at me as if he knows what I am about to do. I decide it was better to not say anything, at least for the moment. Looking over at Rhys for a second, his eyes settle on me again. "Maybe later, after a few drinks."

"You know I don't go out drinking with you two." I frown, slightly uncomfortable, the air feeling heavy.

"Well, what are you gonna do about that?" Shaun shrugs again, before placing the final remains of his sandwich in his mouth and chewing it, all the while continuing to look at me. Finally, he swallows, and says, "Anyways, we better get back to work soon. Can't spend too long on breaks, after all."

Even after both Rhys and Shaun leave, I continue to sit there for a little while afterwards, alone with my own thoughts. I am unsure sure what exactly just happened, but I am fairly certain Shaun has just shut me off completely from learning the truth. Even though he offered to tell it after a few drinks, it isn't as if it is something I would ever go and do, and he knows it. So why had he phrased it in such a way?

It isn't until after work had ended and the two of them left to go drink at the pub, did I truly realize just what he that had meant by all of that.

~

I walk home by myself the same way that I came. It is already night by the time that I get out of work, and as I wave goodbye to Rhys and Shaun, I am left alone with my own thoughts. My eyes are focused on where I was walking, not bothering to look up and see the world around me, the sound of my feet hitting the pavement which each tap of my shoes.

It is a bitter pill to swallow, that Shaun doesn't seem to trust me – or likely, that he just doesn't consider me worthy of hearing the truth. Perhaps it didn't have any deeper meaning, and it had actually been a genuine offer to go out with the two of them, but that isn't the way I had taken it. Besides, the way he had looked at me when he said it made it all abundantly clear.

However, even though he doesn't want me to hear what he was going to say, I can still speculate to myself what Shaun had meant. Maybe he doesn't want me to know, but I could figure it out on my own, and then surprise him with it. Yes, that would be rather enjoyable, I decide. To shove it in his face like that would get to him. It'd show him for rejecting me like that.

So, what had Shaun meant exactly when he said that 'he could feel it'? It wasn't as if it was a physical touch, he had made that clear enough, but how could he feel it when it wasn't even real to begin with? There surely is an explanation to this which didn't need resorting to an urban legend to explain it.

There is so little to go on, though. The best I can reason from what he had said was that it had something more to do with its presence — so perhaps it was something that Shaun had confused for it? Yet what could that have been? Had he simply believed there was someone behind him, and assumed that it was the case?

Maybe there was someone behind him, but it had just been a normal human being. Because he had never looked back to check what it actually was, his mind refused to accept any answer except that it was a monster. Without seeing it for himself, there were infinite possibilities for what might have been behind Shaun — but because he hadn't done so, it was impossible to say which one it might have been. What exactly he 'felt' that night was therefore near impossible to rationally determine unless I had more information from him, which he had refused to tell me.

How annoying. Perhaps my respect for Shaun is misplaced. I would have to change how I act around him from now on. Maybe with Rhys, too, now that I was thinking about it. He seemed far too eager to agree with Shaun after everything was said and done. I had a feeling that Rhys would be walking to work alone tomorrow, if I could do anything to help it.

As I walk past a group of university students on their way to some pub or club or party — I don't really care which it was, to be honest — I feel instinctually repulsed by them. It is exactly these types of people, I believe, who spread such stories and make them take hold in the local population. Students who don't have anything better to do than to make things up in order to explain their frights induced by alcohol and drugs and whatever else, leaving their senses vulnerable to be manipulated and confused. It really was annoying just how many of them there were like that, loud and ignorant, taking up for too much space when walking around without care for their surroundings.

So why does Shaun believe in them? What makes their point of view better than mine? What kind of appeal does it have to believe in something so obviously false?

Fables, as far as I understand them, are used to teach children important lessons, and to keep them away from dangerous situations. This makes sense, and I had never had any need to question this.

Then what about the urban legend? What sort of use do they have in society? Why are they spread — often times not by parents in order to dissuade their children from committing dangerous acts, but by otherwise rational-minded adults? These are questions that I am not so sure of the answers to, yet.

Why does Shaun think he encountered something like what is described in that urban legend on Owens Road? Even though he is even older than me, he has convinced himself that he has had experienced something which should not be possible. I always assumed that the older someone became, the more inclined they were to let go of such beliefs, but clearly, I am mistaken.

Exiting the High Street, I walk along the main road for a short while before taking the left when it forks at a roundabout, which would eventually lead on to Owens Road. It is the same way I go every other workday, and I hadn't ever had anything strange happen to me in all my years I had been living here. It is just another sign, in my mind, how this urban legend is just that — a legend. Make-believe. A farce. Something which is not, and could never be, real.

Such stories cease to have any meaningful use for a person once they become an adult. Anyone who clings to such stories, such as Shaun, are only deluding themselves into thinking the world was far more fantastical than it actually is.

These sorts of things are supposed to be grown out of once you exit childhood. Even as a teenager, if you hold onto such beliefs, you are looked at with scorn. This will only continue the older you get, and the more people let go of superstitions and begin to accept reality. There was no magic, there were no fairies. Accepting this is all simply a part of growing up.

Yet, people still choose to believe in such things despite it all, and this is truly beyond my understanding. It makes me scratch my head how exactly they are able to stand it all, when the world was defined by rules and limitations that clearly went against what they seemed to be claiming was reality.

Seeing these sorts of individuals leaves a bitter taste in my mouth, especially when I see otherwise respectable people convincing themselves of their own delusions. After all, what use did it have to do something like this? It was pointless. All it does is make others cringe at what such a person would have to say and look at them with distrust. After all, if they can't distinguish the difference between reality and fiction, just how trustworthy are they?

This is, of course, why I believe myself to be better than them. I am proud to say that I am a rational-minded individual. I view everything with a realistic outlook and refuse to accept explanations unless they are backed by calculable and observable reasoning. It is the way I live my life, and the principles which define them. I would never think to betray them, no matter what – even if my life were to depend on it.

This is the reason why I am better than Shaun, who decided to believe in the unnatural due to his own perceptions without even attempting to verify them. This is why I am better than Rhys, who flits between what he believes depending on who he is with. This is why I was better than so many people, who live their lives full of superstition, for the sole purpose of living in a world which seemed so much better than it actually was.

Perhaps I am being a bit rude, though. It isn't as if I hate people like this, after all. It was more that I find them rather misguided, and that frustrates me, making it a bother to interact with them.

Looking up, I look over the street that seems to have become the subject of both my fascination and derision. How such a quaint, suburban street would spawn such a story is beyond me — it is far more fitting for something inside the city, in my mind. I can see light shining faintly outside of people's homes, yet curiously all of the houses had their curtains drawn, as if they didn't want to look out on the street.

As I walk, I notice it is rather quiet, although that was not unusual, especially when I am on my way back from work. Yet, even then, it seemed almost a little bit unnatural, although that might have been exaggerating it a little. In fact, it seems almost as if the only thing that I can hear is...

I stop dead in my tracks, and the noise stops too.

What was it I had just heard?

As far as I can see in front of me, the road was abandoned — not a single soul present. The only thing illuminating the pathways themselves are streetlights, each one slightly different in intensity to varying degrees because of use. Yet it isn't anything that I can see in front of me that could have been the source of it, surely.

It might have been my imagination, but- no, I had definitely heard something behind me.

What was it that I had just heard?

I try to strain my ears to listen, to catch that sound again, but I can't hear anything at all. Nothing at all — not even noises that I would have otherwise not registered, such as birds or cars going past the roads on the adjacent blocks. Even the sound of my own breathing feels quieter than normal. It was as if the entire world had been muted, so that the intensity of what I had heard is only enhanced.

What was it that I had just heard?

I try to rationalize my own thoughts, trying to take into account all of the factors that might explain it. Maybe I had imagined it, or misheard something else, or unconsciously registered it as such. It isn't possible, after all, for me to have heard it.

What was it that I had just heard?

I know I should simply shake off this absurd feeling and just continue walking home, but I am almost afraid to take another step forward. What if I hear it again? What if they were right, after all? My heart feels like it is about to burst from the pressure, yet I can't even hear it beating.

I just need to continue walking. Lifting my foot has never felt more exhausting, as if it is being weighed down to the ground in order to keep me from going forwards, because if I took another step and heard what I thought I had heard then everything would be wrong in the world. Yet despite all my hesitation and worry it is over in an instant as my foot hits the concrete sidewalk, another step forward and-

-I hear the sound of another footstep right behind me.

There is no mistaking it. It was only after a small delay, but I had definitely heard it.

A shiver courses through my body when I realized it, the hairs on my skin standing up. It feels ridiculous, to be this afraid of something that wasn't supposed to be real, which I had believed to definitively not be real — yet here I stand all the same, terrified of it.

It sounds so close, too. As if it was right behind me, right at my back. Isn't it supposed to start from a distance? How didn't I notice it until now? Was I so caught up in my own thoughts that I hadn't paid it any mind? Panicking, so many questions seem to rush through my mind, yet I can't even give any of them a decent answer before another question seems to pop up, displacing the previous one.

I am being ridiculous. I know this. It feels frustrating that I was being caught up in this. I know this shouldn't be real, yet my body is still reacting in a way that I can't explain, and I am perceiving things which should not have been possible. I am experiencing the fable that I want to deny so badly.

I don't drink, I don't smoke, I don't do drugs, for this exact reason. So that my senses can remain unfiltered and pure, and to keep my mind clear. Yet now it is being tainted by something that I can't control. What I am experiencing shouldn't have been possible for someone as sober as me. So why is it happening? Why is my mind playing such a cruel trick on me, now of all times?

Perhaps it is the case that thinking about it so much has led me to unconsciously attempt to replicate the situation that has captured my attentions for all of today. I had been thinking about it the entire way home, after all — far more than I would ever have given it mind before. Because I was keeping it in my thoughts, I subconsciously ended up replicated the situation within my own mind. Now that I am aware of this, and having registered my subconscious thoughts, it should no longer be affecting me. If I take another step, I would see that-

-I hear the sound of another footstep right behind me.

It sounds far closer this time, almost as if it was right behind me. How could it seem so much closer if I hadn't moved at all between the time I took my last step and just now? It was almost as if it replaced the spot I had just moved away from, its presence taking where my foot had one stood, as if it was matching my own footsteps.

How I know this, I am not exactly sure. This feeling isn't based on anything rational. It is an instinctual awareness of the space between me and whatever is behind me. I can feel that

there was something there — but what was it?

Perhaps this is what Shaun had meant when he said that he could 'feel' it. It is unlike anything I had ever experienced before. Vividly, I am able to sense that there is something behind me, yet I am unable to understand what it is or what it is doing. So long as I do not look behind me, it could be doing anything or nothing at all. Yet until I look, it would remain an indistinguishable presence that I cannot shake away.

It is as if I was being stalked by Schrödinger's Cat, and it is playing a game with me. I suppose I must have been the mouse, then, if this analogy is to be completed. It is frustrating just how helpless this all made me, in the end. Yet, still, incessantly, I am unable to let go of this lingering thought in my mind.

What exactly is standing behind me right now?

If it is nothing, then I am correct about everything, and they are wrong. If it is something, they are correct about everything, and I was the one who is wrong. It is as simple as that. In this moment, the rational and the irrational are facing off against each other, to see which one will end up the victor.

Adrenaline seems to be rushing through my veins, and I can feel the cold sweat pouring down body, making my shirt cling to my skin from how wet it is becoming. I have never experienced anything quite like this before, never anything quite as exhilarating as these few moments. How long have I been standing here, I wonder? A few seconds? A minute? Ten? It is quite hard to keep track of time when all of my senses are focused on what is or is not behind me.

Even if I don't look, what would I do? Continue walking, all the while knowing that there was something there, right behind me, and try not to look and see what it is? To do so while still being unable to escape the sound of my own footsteps following me, no matter how fast I might have tried to walk, or run, makes me dread going forwards. It might have been what Shaun had done, but it isn't an option for me.

No, I decided then and there on what I would do.

In all honesty, despite my own bravado, the very thought of looking behind me is a terrifying one. Every instinct in my body is trying to tell me to let it all go and admit defeat, to rush to the safety of my home and to forget any of this ever happened. To never speak a word of this to anyone, for fear of being viewed as being beneath others. To not, under any circumstances, look behind me, and to see what was behind my back, and to observe the truth.

A part of me wants to do all of this, despite myself. Maybe a small part of me really does believe in this urban legend after all, if this is what my instincts was telling me to do. I am not sure why this thought came out, now of all times, yet it is one I couldn't deny held some amount of weight.

Yet at the same time, I know I can't do any of that.

I can't continue home. I can't ignore what was behind me. I can't admit defeat. It isn't possible, for me, as a person, to continue living if I do any of these things.

I need to know. I need to know what was behind me. If I am to understand what was happening, I need to see it with my own two eyes. I have decided that this was a necessity. Even if all my instincts are telling me that I should just ignore it and continue walking, I need to know.

I need to look. I need to see if I was right or not. I need to prove that they were wrong, and I was right.

I turn to look behind me and-

Printed in Great Britain
by Amazon

86384541R00068